# HI I'M A SOCIAL DISEASE

## ANDERSEN PRUNTY

GRINDHOUSE PRESS

Published by Grindhouse Press
POB 292644
Dayton, OH  45429
www.grindhousepress.com

*Hi I'm a Social Disease: Horror Stories*
Grindhouse Press #007
ISBN-13: 978-0-9849692-0-3
ISBN-10: 0984969209


This book is a work of fiction.

Cover design copyright © 2011 by Brandon Duncan
www.corporatedemon.com

Cover photograph © 2011 by Michel Omar Berrospé

hi

i'm a social

disease

# Also by Andersen Prunty

*Sunruined: Horror Stories (forthcoming)*
*The Driver's Guide to Hitting Pedestrians*
*Fuckness*
*The Sorrow King*
*Slag Attack*
*My Fake War*
*Morning is Dead*
*The Beard*
*Jack and Mr. Grin*
*Zerostrata*
*The Overwhelming Urge*

# Contents

# ROOM 29



She moved into Room 29. That was the one right over mine. I wish she had moved somewhere else.

The first time I saw her, I was coming home from the store, a bottle of whiskey wrapped in a paper bag clutched in my right hand. She had three cardboard boxes in front of her and was bent over one of them, lifting it. Dirty strawberry blond hair hung over the right side of her face so my gaze drifted lower to the skin between her blue stockings and thin yellow sundress. I tried not to let it stop me but I had to stare. She finally hoisted the box up against her chest and turned, startled, to see me standing only a couple of feet away.

"I'd like to help you," I said. "But I can't... I just can't."

"Yeah," she said in little more than a resigned whisper. Her face was thin and pretty. Everyone was thin these days but most people who were left weren't very pretty. She turned her back to me and started into the shell of the building.

I stood there until she disappeared into the darkness. There hadn't been a door since before I moved in. I took a deep breath and looked up at the ashy gray sky. I couldn't remember the last time I'd seen the sun. I couldn't remember the last time I'd seen a pretty face. Once I was sure I wouldn't run into her again, I went into the building and into my room, Room 19.

I walked through the trash strewn about the floor, flipped the television on, and sat down on the wasted, moldy couch. I put the bottle, still in the bag, on the saggy upright cardboard box that served as an end table. Upstairs, I heard her clunk the box down on the floor. Static flickered across the television. There weren't any stations. Electricity, for now. Electricity was useless. It would keep the refrigerator running but there wasn't anything to put in it. It would keep the television going but there wasn't anything to watch. It would keep the lights on but, Christ, who wanted to see?

I heard her shuffling back down the hall, just outside my door, to get another box. Three boxes was pretty impressive. That was a lot of stuff to own. No one owned anything anymore. Things were just status symbols anyway and now there wasn't anyone to impress. She was probably wondering why I wouldn't help her. Or maybe she wasn't. One tended not to wonder about much. We'd seen it all. All of our nightmares had blazed to life right in front of us so if a stranger didn't offer to help you carry a few boxes, well, she was probably just thankful I didn't drag her into the building and have my way with her. Because I could have. The law was too busy to concern itself with something like rape.

The truth was that I was afraid to go toward the back of the building. And you had to go to the back to get to the stairs. The landlord, Mr. Grangely, lived back there. Until the girl showed up, I was the only other person in the building. He didn't charge rent but if you died in his building he would cook you up and eat you. Sometimes I think he helped that death along. I never went near him by choice.

I looked at the unwrapped bottle.

The screams were coming on. I could feel them way down in my guts. My ma used to say that was a demon. She said it explained the way I acted much of the time. I didn't believe in demons. I thought Ma was full of shit, rest her soul.

I knew what happened if I didn't let the screams out. I had to. It was like a release valve. But it was going to be embarrassing now. Now that there was someone besides a cannibal to hear me. What would she think? Did it matter what she thought? Probably not.

The screams came on all of a sudden. I dug my fingernails into the arms of the chair, reached down deep past my diaphragm and dragged the first scream out. It was long and brutal and painful. Twelve more followed it. I screamed until I could taste blood in the back of my mouth. Then, with sweaty, shaky hands, I opened the bottle, tossing the bag and the cap on the floor, and dumped the first swallow into my mouth.

Ah, the numbing fire.

There was a knock on the door.

I didn't say anything. My voice was gone. The screams always stole my voice, not that it usually mattered.

"Are you all right?"

I took another slug of the whiskey and doubled over, resisting the urge to run to the door and throw it open. But I didn't because I knew it could only end in pain.

"You okay in there?"

She twisted the knob but it was locked. When sharing the house with a cannibal of questionable ethics, one does not leave the door unlocked.

"I'm right upstairs if you need anything, kay?"

Then she was shuffling away, back that dark hall toward the stink of Grangely's room and up those rickety stairs. Right above me. I heard her moving around. Opening boxes. I sat in the chair, drinking and watching static until night fell.

I must have dozed off or passed out in the chair. When I came to I could hear her crying upstairs. It was so loud it sounded almost like she had her face pressed to the floor. It was the most melancholy sound I'd ever heard. I must have still been half asleep because I imagined her tears seeping through the floorboards, falling through the rancid stale air like drops of seawater, hitting me in the face, trickling into my mouth. I drifted back off, my belly full of whiskey, sadness, and longing.

The next morning I woke up stiff and sweaty. The days were like this. Most of them were cold but there were these occasional sticky, humid days. I didn't know what season it was. I'd had a calendar once but lost it and then stopped caring. I stood up, stretched, went into a corner and pissed. You get used to the smell. The whiskey bottle was empty. I don't know why I didn't just piss in the whiskey bottles. Whiskey in. Whiskey out. Now I'd have to go to the store. I suppose I could just clean the store out but going there gave a sense of routine and normalcy to the day.

I opened the door and saw her standing with her back to it on the other side of the hall. She was looking at the wall of little metal mailboxes. Most of their doors were hanging from the hinges or torn off completely. I quickly shut my door and imagined her turning around. Then I heard her going away. I opened the door again and stepped out, looking at the mailboxes. I looked at the one for 29. She'd added her name to it. Blue marker on a piece of masking tape. Anita Marvel, it said. I ran my fingertips over the tape and thought about that tiny expanse of pale skin above her stocking. I could still smell the fumes from the marker. I thought about my dead wife and my dead kids and wondered if I could ever feel that way about another person. I didn't know.

I came back from the store and hoped to run into her again but she wasn't anywhere to be seen. Her room was silent above me. Sometime in the afternoon I had another bout of the screams and started drinking shortly thereafter. Night fell and I heard Grangely leave the building on one of his excursions. Hunting. That's why he was so fat. He went into the city at least once a week and returned with fresh feral children, wild animals, whatever he could catch and cut down in the dark back alleys of the city. They were always dead when he brought them back. I don't think I could have stood it if they were still alive. What he did was ghoulish enough without having to listen to some poor innocent struggle as he took them out of this rotten world.

The girl, Anita, began moving around shortly after he left. She walked back and forth across the floor. It squeaked and wobbled. What was there to walk back and forth to? What reason was there to even move? I thought about going up to her room, knocking on her door, introducing myself, but I was pretty sure I was too drunk to stand up. After a long while I heard her settle down and begin that weeping again. Some people scream. Some people weep. The sound of her weeping made me sad but there was something about it more human and beautiful than I had heard in a very long time.

The days and nights continued like this. She became part of the routine, as unchanging as the cloud-covered sky. But I never forgot about her. I longed for her. That became a constant too. That became part of the routine. I watched her check her mail each morning, always in that dingy yellow sundress and blue stockings. She never received anything. I listened to her pace and cry at night. I thought about going up there all the time. I should have. At the very least, she needed warned about Grangely. She needed to know what it was he did, what would become of her if she happened to die here.

I never went.

One evening, something banged against my door and I snapped out of my drowse. My hands had gone numb and I thought I was blind in my left eye. I flexed my hands and blinked. I stood up and went to the door. I opened it but there wasn't anyone or anything there. I thought Grangely had accidentally bumped into it on his way out. But I could hear him at the back of the hall. I looked at him. He was down on all fours, sniffing. I looked down. If he was sniffing the floor there was a good chance something was there. Something was. A thin trail of blood.

Anita was my first thought. Grangely and I were accounted for. The blood trail led outside. I turned to face Grangely. "Get back in your room, Fatass." There wasn't any need to shout. No noise. No other people.

He stood up. He was a large man, tall and robust in a skeletal age.

"You don't boss me," he said. "I'm the fuckin landlord."

"I know what you do. If I wanted, I could tell someone. There aren't any landlords anymore. There aren't any titles anymore. Just people."

"You'll fuckin get yours." We stared at each other for a few uncomfortable seconds before he turned and went back toward his room, slamming his door shut behind him.

I turned back toward the opening of the building, staring out at the dark milky night. I didn't see her. The trail of blood was thin at first and then, by the time I had reached the curb, it had tapered off into sporadic splashes. I didn't want to venture out any farther. Not at night. I thought about yelling for her but I couldn't bring myself to do it. She didn't even know me. I looked back down at the final splash of blood. I'd never be able to find her that way.

I looked into the surrounding darkness and took a deep breath. Loss was nothing new. I wasn't even close to her. If I started grieving for people I didn't know then I had a whole life of grief in front of me. Every day people died. Every day people disappeared.

I went back into the building. Back into my room. Despite having drunk an entire bottle of whiskey, unconsciousness wouldn't come back. I began to wish I had stockpiled it so I would have something else to dive into.

I had never experienced the night like this before. It was maddening. I sat in the chair, watching the static and listening to hear if she ever came back. Toward dawn the electricity started flickering and I knew this was the beginning of the end. Not that it mattered to me anyway. I hadn't allowed myself to become reliant on any of the appliances. I only kept the television on because I thought I should use something.

Once it was full on morning, I went to the store to get some more whiskey. I almost passed out on the way there. How was it that I could stay up all night and now that the air was bright I felt like I would fall asleep if I shut my eyes? I was so tired I felt sick.

I made it back to the building, put the whiskey on the cardboard end table, and screamed myself to sleep.


She was the first thing I thought about when I woke up. I had to do it. I had to go up to her room to see if she was okay. I took a slug of the whiskey to fortify my nerves and began the long walk down the hall and toward the stairs. The stink, as I drew closer to Grangely's, was increasingly nauseating. It was one thing to be a fucking cannibal but you'd think he'd clean up after himself. He didn't have to be so unashamed about it.

I climbed the dark and rickety staircase, waiting for my foot to drop through one of the boards, until I reached the second floor.

Down the hall to Room 29.

The door was ajar. I pushed it inward. It smelled like flowers and meat inside. Something light and pretty over something black and rotten. I didn't want to snoop but, well, there wasn't anything better to do. My conscience wasn't what it used to be. Besides, it didn't look like there were a lot of things to snoop through, anyway.

The three boxes she had brought with her were turned on their sides on the floor at the bottom of the far wall. Notebooks were lined up on top of them. They looked swollen and puffy like they had been left out in the rain. Her room had a bed and I wondered how many people had died in it. On top of the bed sat another notebook. It was the old kind of composition book with the black and white, vaguely bovine, pattern.

I really shouldn't have.

But I had to. Because there wasn't anything else to do and, I rationalized with myself, if she never came back, this would be a way to remember her. I imagined what I was about to go through was a journal. How could the pages of a journal live if no one ever reads them? I knew it was more than that. I knew I was going to read it because I wanted her. I wanted to possess some small part of her and if I was too much a coward to try and get inside her physically then this was how I'd do it mentally.

I opened up the notebook.

I expected to see the hasty scrawl of handwriting. That's what a journal was, wasn't it? That's not what I saw at all. It was an oblong, crusty, crimson-black mass. It looked like a scab. I flipped the pages with a mixture of disgust and intrigue. More of the same. One per page. I closed the notebook and went over to the other notebooks arranged on the boxes. The first two I opened were empty. Perhaps those were for the future. But the rest of them were filled with more of the same. Scabs. I was sure of it. These were diaries of scabs. I ran my fingers over them. The ones on the boxes were drier, older. Bits of them had flaked off and were smashed between the pages. Some of them came away on my fingertip. I stuck it in my mouth. It tasted like blood, come back to life on my tongue. I put the diary I presently held back on the cardboard box and arranged them as they were originally, neat and orderly. Then I went back to the bed and flipped through that one. This must be the latest one. The scabs inside this one seemed fresher, hanging on to the blue-lined pages with more intensity.

I sat down on the bed and continued to flip through it, running my fingers over them and wondering what the point of this was. Really, what was the point of anything anymore?

I thought of her melancholy weeping. Was that what it sounded like when she cut herself? Did she do that to let some of the pain out? I had dreamed about reading her diary and possessing a little of what was inside of her but this was greater than I could ever have imagined. I probably stayed in her room for two hours. Then my insides were crying to pour out so I left the diary where I had found it, went back down to my room, released myself to the screams, and drank myself into a coma.

When I woke up it was dark and all the electricity had gone. That made it official, I guessed. The end was here.


The next two days continued like all the ones before it only now I spent a bit of time in Anita's room, lost in her diaries and wondering if she would ever come back. Then, after being gone for four days, she did.

Unfortunately, I was busy looking through her diary when she entered the room. A rare thunderstorm was upon us, turning the dim afternoon nearly nighttime black. She startled me but I immediately realized I had been caught.

"What are you doing?" she said.

I held up the diary. "Looking through this."

Her left arm was missing below the elbow. A yellowish bandage covered the stump.

"What happened to your arm?"

"You know... You know what I've been doing up here, don't you?"

"I think I do."

"I cut myself too deep. I had to go look for help. I don't want to die, you know? It just feels like something I have to do." She paused and held her right arm up to her chest. "Like your screaming."

"Yes."

It was then I decided I was going to kill her. She had crossed the room and was arranging her past diaries. Her dirty sundress was up above her blue stockings again and it was then I decided everything was hopeless. I would kill her and keep her for my own because I couldn't stand the thought of that beast Grangely gnawing on her. Her being in the apartment was something. She was the promise.

The promise of everything missing. I would kill her and then I would kill myself. I realized I would never see her in anything but that yellow sundress and blue stockings, the screams would never go away, the electricity would never come back, the whiskey would run out, and the sun was never going to show its face again. I had already done some very bad things and the dead world was rotting around me.

I turned my attention back to the diary I held in my hand.

"You shouldn't just read people's diaries right in front of them," she said.

"I know." I closed it and stared out the darkened window at the nothing darkness outside. "I came up here to warn you."

"Warn me? You didn't need a reason to come up here. I'm surprised it took you this long. What were you going to warn me about?"

"Grangely."

"Who's that?" she whispered from behind me.

"The landlord."

"The landlord?"

"Yes, he lives downstairs."

"No one lives downstairs except you."

I laughed. "You've had to have seen him. The fat guy. The one who smells so bad. Anyway, when the tenants die, he eats them. And he makes excursions out into the city at night. He brings back all kinds of things."

"Things? Like people?"

"Yeah. Sometimes."

"That's horrible. That's how I lost my sister. At least, that's what everybody suspects."

I felt her weight on the other side of the bed. I thought about turning around but didn't want to spoil everything. I could imagine her hot breath on the back of my neck. It had been so long since I had felt anything like that. Would I actually get to possess her?

"That's a shame," I said.

# Room 11

"It is. She used to go to this little corner store for candy. She went there just about every day. Usually she took a grownup along with her but you know how candy is... It's like an addiction after a while. Somebody got her. Apparently, he got quite a few people. He was keeping them in a deep freezer of the store's cellar. He would keep them there and go back every day, eating little pieces of them, cooking them on a portable grill in the store's office. They sifted through the ash and found Sis's earrings."

She said that and I had an image of the cellar. The owners had lived above the store and had apparently used the cellar for their own storage. They had died a long time ago.

"Guess he's shit out of luck now that the electricity's finally gone," she said.

"Yeah," I mouthed but my throat had closed up.

She leaned over me and I felt her hot breath on the back of my neck and cold steel pressed to the front. I looked down and saw the handle. It was the kind of straight razor no one had used in a very long time, even before the end of the world.

"I always wondered why you were always screaming until I saw that. We've been looking for you for a very long time. You know, most everybody else has really come together. I've seen people do things I didn't know they were capable of. Good things."

"You can kill me," I said. "I deserve it." What else could I say? This would be the best way to go. Visions of lynch mobs filled my head. There was no point in fighting back. Even if she was a one-armed girl.

"I'm not going to do that. We can use you."

Outside, I noticed lights from a car. I still wasn't entirely sure of all the things I had done but I knew they were bad and I knew it was me who had done them. Within the next few seconds the room was swarming with people, most of them tired and hungry and hostile. They were not very gentle with me.

They brought me to a hospital. It's a hospital for some, a

laboratory for others, and a prison to many. They never told me anything directly but, since I was now human waste, they talked about me like I wasn't there so I heard a lot of things. They had discovered the nature of the plague. They thought they were close to figuring out how to reverse it. It was the only way. To reverse it. To regrow what had rotted on our insides. No one used the word soul. I was recruited.

I've become an experiment. I sit writing this with a third hand growing out of my forehead. It's all a sick joke. They wanted to see if I could develop my dexterity with this new hand. I wanted to ask about Anita. I wanted to ask if she still kept her scab diary. I wanted to ask them if any of them knew why she kept that diary in the first place... You have to admire the human spirit—we'll continue building things just so someone else can watch them fall. I wish I could put the pen down and run my fingertips over Anita's scabs because that was what we were leaving behind and that was what we were working so hard to build. Bloody crusts over wounds.

I haven't seen her again.

Now I sit here and keep my own diary, written in the pus from a hundred different infections.

# MARKET ADJUSTMENT

1.

*New York—October 28, 1929*

"A hotdog, mister?"

"Got any money?"

Myron Barnes patted his tattered overcoat, knowing he didn't have any money. He caught the vendor's eye and tossed his hands out to the side. "I ain't had no money for days. Thought I might find somethin." Myron turned away. "I understand. You got a business you're tryin to run."

"Hold up now. I think I can spare one."

Myron turned back around to face him. Their eyes stayed locked and the vendor's motions were mechanical, assembling and wrapping the hotdog, handing it across the cart to Myron.

"Jeez, thanks mister. When I make my fortune I'll make sure to pay you. Consider this a loan." He held up the hotdog before taking a big hungry bite of it.

"I wouldn't count on that. Don't think nobody's makin money

today. Head down to Wall Street, you'll see a whole lotta panic. That is… unless you got somewhere else to go."

"I think you and me both know I don't."

"Enjoy. I think a whole lotta people's about to join you."

Myron turned his back on the vendor with a dismissive wave. He took another bite of the hotdog and headed toward Wall Street. The vendor's words stung him. Had it become that obvious he lived on the street?

Luckily, Myron thought, he still had his youth and some vestige of his looks. Maybe it was just his eyes. Somehow he was able to compel people to do things for him. Maybe they just saw poverty and desperation. So, yeah, he lived on the street, but it wasn't hard to find some girl to take him in for the night. More often than not, he had a place to sleep. And he had the Enclave.

He crouched down in front of a sewer grate and took one last, longing look at the remainder of the hotdog before dropping it down. He rose and wiped his hands on his filthy pants, his stomach now gurgling pleasantly as it broke down the food.

He breathed in the crisp October air and turned onto Wall Street.

It was choked with panic. People shouting in disbelief, running hands through their hair, and clutching their pockets like something could reach in and take whatever was left right out. A palpable buzz binding everyone together.

Who were these captains of industry?

Materialistic money worshippers, Myron thought. No one knew which gods they worshipped anymore so these people had chosen to worship their bank accounts. They had built a house of cards and now, watching a man's hat fly off as he kicked the tires of a nearby Nash with great fury, that house of cards had fallen. This was the aftermath.

Myron did his best not to smile. Not that anyone would have noticed.

Join me, he thought. Join me here at the bottom of the world.

A rain of glass exploded from above, followed by a heavy

wooden office chair. The crowd gathered on the sidewalk backed out into the street and craned their heads upward.

A collective gasp. A man flying through the air, framed against the gorgeous blue sky, his jacket and pants flapping as he clawed at the empty space around him.

He hit the ground in an explosion of bone fragments and gore. Myron crossed his arms to shield his eyes. A woman to his right screamed. An eyeball had slapped against the lapel of her jacket, and she did a weird little dance as it sluggishly slid down before plopping onto the greasy asphalt.

Myron felt blood spattered against his palms. He held his hands out in front of him to examine them, the gesture of begging all too familiar.

A hundred dollar bill rested wetly in each palm.

He casually wrapped his hands around the bills and slid them into each of his pants pockets before disappearing down the nearest alley.

2.

The grimy alley smelled like piss. Behind him, savage screams and squealing tires. It was like a switch had been thrown and every siren in the city now roared around him. He looked up at the endless blue sky. A thick black cloud drifted over, sealing the entire financial district in shades of gray and black. No more blue sky.

Toward the end of the alley, he saw what he was hoping to see. A service entrance door. A place for the dirty people to enter. A place for the under people. A man staggered out of the door. He wasn't an under person. He wore a dark pin-striped suit and looked slightly disheveled. He turned to his right, toward the hungry throng out on Wall Street and, noticing Myron, said, "Hey! Hey, buddy!" He threw out his right arm and grabbed Myron's left, jostling it. Then he retracted his hand and wiped it on the thigh of his trousers.

"I ain't your buddy," Myron said.

This didn't seem to faze the man. He blinked his eyes and shook his head. "No hard feelings, buddy. Times are tough for everyone. You know, I got a boat. Docked in the harbor. It's a fine boat. The *Black Swan*. You wanna see my boat?"

"I don't think I got time. I gotta get inside and do some things."

The guy chuffed and straightened his lapels. Myron wondered if maybe he was drunk.

"Fuck man. I'm gonna go get on my boat and sail it to... hell, anywhere but here. Then I'm gonna come back and everything's gonna be over." The man pulled a flask from his pocket and unscrewed the top, belting it back and answering Myron's question. "This shit's gonna blow over." He brandished the still open flask at Myron. "Just you wait and see. But it's gonna get real ugly before it does."

Myron nodded and made for the door. The guy moved to stand in his way. Myron grabbed the flask and threw it toward the far end of the alley. It clanged as it skidded down the asphalt and the man ran after it. Myron opened the service entrance door and walked into the Chambers National Bank building.

3.

Not surprisingly, he didn't run into any service workers as he took the stairs down to the basement. On the whole, they tended to be smarter than the people whose toilets they cleaned. They had probably taken off at the first sign of trouble. Sick kids. Sick relatives. Funerals. Viewings. Not feeling well. Appointment. The excuses were endless.

Once in the basement, he went immediately to the fuse box. It didn't take him long to find what he was looking for. The fuses for the forty-third floor. He wondered briefly why the building was named after the Chambers National Bank when they only occupied part of one floor. He hoped this was the floor he needed. That was where the checks had been addressed to, and later not addressed to.

*Be best if it's done in the dark.* Mama Hodap's voice, sweet as sugar, rolled around in his head.

Unscrewing the fuses, he thought about the two hundred dollars in his pockets and wondered if that would have changed anything.

Maybe some things were inevitable. Maybe everyone built his own house of cards. He unscrewed the final fuse and, because he was alone and because he didn't think anyone would hear him, he screamed.

He quit when he tasted blood on the back of his tongue.

4.

He took the stairs back up to the lobby. He supposed he could have taken the elevator all the way up to 43 but he didn't want to go up there as an under man. He wanted to go up there the same as everybody else. In the brightly lighted, scrubbed clean lobby he looked toward the elevator and decided he wanted to look outside again. He had been told this was going to be a monumental day and he wanted to see just how monumental it was to be.

For him, he knew it was going to be huge. But what about for everyone else?

He wandered over to the front of the lobby. It was hard to look casual. Through the glass he saw the storm dimmed street.

There were even more people out there now.

The man who had been kicking his car was still kicking his car. His shoe had deteriorated, his foot a red pulp.

A crowd of people stood around the remains of the jumper. The ambulance and police had arrived and were busy trying to shoo some enterprising dogs away. The medics looked at the remains like it was a very complicated puzzle. People parted quickly as a car came roaring down the street and continued out of Myron's view.

Myron watched with interest. Their god was dead, at least

temporarily, and it would take them a while before they learned to move on. Maybe they would look for a new god. Mama Hodap had introduced him to a couple of new gods and told him about a whole lot more.

Did he believe in them?

Sure. Mama was an under person. She had no reason to lie. Did he *worship* them? Well, he didn't think he'd ever worship a god again.

He moved toward the elevator so he didn't rouse any suspicion from the dumpy receptionist sitting wide-eyed behind the gleaming counter. He made eye contact with her and nodded. She was lost to the brisk voice of the broadcaster on the radio.

The broadcaster was talking crash.

He was talking bad times.

He was talking depression.

Myron pressed the up button and the elevator opened immediately. He stepped inside and hit the button for 43. He took a deep and shaky breath and ran his hand through his greasy hair. Sometimes to get to the very bottom of things you had to go to the top.

Breathing in the greasy mechanical air of the elevator, he thought about Melinda and Joanie. It had been nearly a year since they had lost their house. But even after that, he had still had *them*. He had still had his family. Six months ago he lost Melinda to TB in a government funded hospital for the poor. Less than a month later he had lost little Joanie to pneumonia. He had been alone and on the street ever since. Even when he went to bed with another woman it was only for the comfort of a bed and a roof over his head. He thought Melinda would understand. Sometime after losing Joanie, he had searched desperately for a purpose since his American dream had become a very cruel nightmare. Those other women, the lifestyle of a carefree tramp, quickly wore on him. Their beds of sweat and perfume, their need and greed and desperation and loneliness could not help him find his purpose.

He blinked the bad memories away before they could sting his eyes with tears and the elevator opened onto a darkened floor.

Before he found his purpose, he'd found the Enclave. And the Enclave had introduced him to Mama Hodap. And she had given him his purpose.

And now the days were getting shorter, and the nights were getting longer, and the god of the new world was dying right in front of him.

5.

He stepped into the wide hallway and left all shreds of a rational world behind.

He didn't mind. It was rationality, cold and clinical, that had gotten him where he was, which was nowhere.

6.

And maybe this was nowhere. *The* Nowhere.

Residual light from the window to his left illuminated the hallway. The elevator closed behind him, sealing him from any impulse to turn back. He knew he could just hit the down button and he also knew he wouldn't be able to live with himself if he did that. He couldn't let the rest of the Enclave down.

A shape moaned to his right and Myron looked down to focus on it.

A man dragged himself along the floor. He wore a dark suit. It was rumpled and torn. His face was swollen and bloodstained. The left leg of his trousers had been ripped away and his leg was severed at the knee. Blood trailed away into the murk behind him.

Myron covered his mouth and fought the urge to throw up. He had prepared himself for this. The black woman in the sewers beneath Harlem had touched him. Mama Hodap. She had looked into him. Amidst thick incense smoke in an unused utility room,

Mama held his hand. Alternately grim and smiling, she had gently folded her hands over his and, in those brief moments, Myron had seen things he begged Mama to take back.

*No, sir.* She shook her head. *Can't unshow somethin already been showed.*

And he knew she was right.

*She* had prepared him for this.

The man on the floor grunted as he took another great heave forward.

Why didn't Myron help him? How *could* he help him? This man was one of the fallen. There would be no rising.

The man pulled himself along until he reached the elevator. Myron continued to watch him. The man seemed to notice Myron for the first time. "Hey, mister?" Down there in the alley he was buddy. Apparently he was mister up here. The man on the floor gagged and strings of blood ran from his mouth. "Think you can help me with the elevator?" He wiped blood from his mouth with the back of his hand and then held it up to the button to demonstrate how he couldn't reach it.

Myron took a couple of steps toward the button and reached over the man to press it.

"Ah, jeez, thanks a lot, mister."

The elevator opened. The man pulled himself halfway in. Before he could make it all the way, the doors shut on his waist, paused, and once again retracted. The man grunted and tried to pull himself faster. Myron reached down to push the man. He didn't know if he wanted to help or if he just wanted the man's blood on his hands.

Myron got him all the way into the elevator and said, "Let this man take my place in the world." With a smirk, he backed away from the elevator.

"What's that..." the man said before the elevator swallowed him.

7.

Now Myron was again left with the meager daylight bleeding into the hallway. Double doors stood at the end opposite the window. He walked toward them, breathing deeply and evenly. From behind the doors he heard glass shattering and people screaming.

CHAMBERS NATIONAL BANK

The name was branded across both doors in the same stylized pattern embossed on the monthly bills he had received. He ran his fingertips across the lettering. While Mama had tried to mentally prepare him for this, he didn't know how one could ever really be prepared for what was about to happen.

*This is just a smokescreen.* She smiled that gentle smile, put her warm brown hand over his. He would have believed anything she told him. *Him and his like are just takin advantage of the chaos. They serve other gods. Oh, they might worship money but you can't serve money. So I feel it's only fair I let you borrow a couple of my gods: Papa Legba and Baron La Croix. They'll need off'rins like any self-respectin deity. And, of course, you don't gotta worship em, you just gotta believe in em.*

Myron had offered the remainder of the hotdog to Papa Legba. The only thing he had left was the money. He pulled the still damp bills from his pockets and placed them in front of the door. He heard a piercing scream and repetitive thump.

"For you, Baron La Croix."

He looked at the bills lying on the floor, expecting them to disappear or something. They didn't. But the blood did. One minute it was there and the next minute the hundred dollar bills looked like they had come fresh from the treasury. Myron picked them up and put them back into his pockets. He stood up and tried the knob on the right. The door wouldn't budge. Already knowing the outcome, he tried the door on his left.

*Papa Legba opens doors.*

What if these weren't the doors he was supposed to open? Would Papa only do something once? Or would he open many doors if Myron asked him to? Better play it safe.

Myron thought he could handle these himself. He went back down the hall about halfway until he came to an emergency station, complete with a fire hose and an ax. He smashed out the glass and grabbed the ax. He held it with both hands, felt its heft, the smooth wood against his palms. Wasting no more time, he stalked to the locked office doors and began smashing at them. All he had to do was bust them a couple of times at the latches and the doors swung open.

8.

As he walked through the doors, another lobby surrounded him. Much like the one on the first floor, only on a smaller scale. A woman lay bound to the receptionist's desk. Her mouth was gagged with dark cloth. She stared crazy eyed at Myron as she struggled against the ropes. Two very large and very black dogs flanked either side of the desk. They growled at Myron. Lean muscles rippled through their haunches.

He heard a man's gruff voice say, "Stay." Then he felt something smack against his head and everything went a little darker than it already was.

9.

It took his eyes a few moments to adjust to the dusky room. His wrists were tied together over his head. He was suspended from the ceiling, his legs bound at the ankles. The room was a very spacious office, fit for the bank president.

The shelves were in disarray, many of them pulled down altogether. A behemoth desk lay toppled on its side. He hung in front of a row of windows. A cold, damp breeze blew in through the ones that had been shattered.

Four people stood watching him from the other side of the

room, slightly to the left of the devastated desk. Two younger men who looked eager and willing to begin their climb up the corporate ladder, a slim blond woman and a stocky, gray-haired man holding a severed lower leg around the ankle.

"I'm looking for Robert Chambers."

The older man barked at him, "Shut the fuck up!" The two goonish men smirked.

Was *this* Robert Chambers, the bank president? It almost had to be. If so, this was the man responsible for foreclosing on his home. This man was partly responsible for the swirling chaos and panic raging through the streets outside.

"Are *you* Robert Chambers?"

"I told you to shut the fuck up!" He turned to the goon on his right. "I thought we had him out of the way but I guess we forgot to do something about that mouth."

"If you're Robert Chambers, I have a message for you from Patrice Hodap…"

In his right hand, he held a stack of papers. He brandished them at Myron.

"I don't know who the fuck that is!"

"You know you're a murderer."

The man stomped up and down like a child throwing a tantrum. "Fuck! Fuck! Fuck! Fuck you! I don't have to listen to you or any other piece of trash from the street."

"I ain't from the street, Mr. Chambers. I'm from a place even farther below."

"I don't care where the fuck you come from." Chambers took a few steps toward him. "I'll cut you loose and you can go back to eating rats in the sewer with that nigger bitch. You have no part in this."

"I'm afraid I do." Myron spit at Chambers, saliva spraying the front of his suit.

Chambers turned his back on Myron and began walking toward the other side of the room.

"Steiner!" Chambers shouted. One of the younger men snapped to attention. "Take these certificates and feed them to this stupid fuck."

"But what if he tries to bite me, sir?"

Chambers drew back the lower leg and smacked Steiner on the shoulder. "You want to join him?"

Steiner took the stock certificates and approached Myron. He struggled against his bonds. He wasn't going to give them the satisfaction of screaming. He made eye contact with Steiner.

"Listen to me," Steiner said. "I'm going to shove these into your mouth and if you make one attempt to bite me you're going out the window. Understand?"

Myron shook his head.

"He's going to bite me! I know it! I can see it in his eyes!"

"If he bites you, we'll break out his teeth and shove them up his prick."

"Open up," Steiner said.

Myron opened his mouth. As Steiner crumpled up the first certificate and pressed it against Myron's lips, Myron gnashed his teeth. Steiner drew back his fist and punched him in the mouth. Myron felt teeth shatter. Steiner shook his hand with pain, dropping the certificate to the floor. It was probably the first time he'd ever hit anyone.

"Lora! Front and center," Chambers barked.

The blond woman approached Chambers. The other man stood to his left, beside a thick-looking door. Myron wondered if it was some kind of safe. It looked like it was made from wood but it could have been lined with steel, for all Myron knew.

Steiner took the first certificate and shoved it into Myron's mouth. Myron gagged and spit the crumpled certificate and some blood back into Steiner's face.

"Little fucker," Steiner said. He bent down and removed a very expensive brown leather shoe.

From the other side of the office, Chambers said, "I need

servicing."

He unzipped his trousers and let them drop to the floor. His erection was enormous.

"No," Lora said.

"What do you mean, 'No'?"

"I won't do it."

"Think about what you're saying. Out there," he gestured to the windows with the leg, "people are going out of their heads because they've lost everything they had. Now I'm offering you whatever it takes to get you down on your knees. How much?"

Steiner balled up another certificate and shoved it into Myron's mouth. This time he took his shoe and crammed the paper to the back of Myron's throat. Myron gagged but the shoe forced his gorge back down and then he had to fight to swallow the paper so he wouldn't choke on it. The aged paper worked its way down his throat. He coughed. Steiner had another certificate ready, shoving it in. It seemed like he'd hit some sort of groove. Myron tasted the old water flavor of the paper, blood, bile, street grime and shoe polish.

"This much?" Chambers produced a stack of bills from the inside pocket of his blazer. He peeled off a couple and threw them in Lora's face.

"I won't."

"This much?" He threw a couple more bills at her.

"This much?" He ground a wad into her face.

Myron wondered why she stood there and took this. Why didn't she turn and run? Why hadn't she run a while ago when Chambers had undoubtedly blown some kind of gasket? Maybe this wasn't abnormal. Maybe he always acted like this.

He dropped the entire stack on the floor in front of her.

"Still no?"

"Never."

"Fuck it. Money's worthless anyway."

Chambers kicked the stack away and it exploded in a greenish flutter. He sat the severed leg onto the floor. He ripped off his jacket and his shirt, finished stripping off his pants, standing stocky and naked. Through Myron's watery eyes, he looked like a predatory animal. Chambers picked the leg back up.

"Todd!"

"Yes, sir!" the remaining man bellowed.

"Shit on this stack of money."

"Yes, sir!"

Todd came out of his stoic stupor to walk over, drop his pants, and squat over the stack of loose bills.

"I'll just take what I want," Chambers said.

Myron choked down another certificate and coughed, "Lora!"

The woman turned to him as though she hadn't even realized there was anyone else in the room until now.

"Run!"

"I can't. The dogs." She stood there whimpering, looking down at Todd and the stack of money with disgust, bringing her arms instinctively over her chest.

Was she just hoping the madness would suddenly end?

Chambers snapped out with the leg and caught her on the side of the head with a meaty *thunk*. Lora fell to her right, bloody hair sticking to her face. Myron didn't know if the blood came from her or the leg.

He couldn't watch this. He had to do something. He pulled his knees up to his chest and savagely kicked out at Steiner as he reached toward him with another certificate. He planted the kick squarely in Steiner's chest. He staggered backward, caught himself, and was on Myron in a second, catching him across the face with the hard sole of his shoe. Myron went dizzy with the bolt of pain and the violent swinging of the rope. He wondered what he was suspended from. How easy it would be to break.

He heard fabric rip and Lora scream.

The office smelled like shit and vomit and blood. And beneath it all, the smell of old money and endless comfort.

He swung around, staring out over the city through the busted window and now back into the office. His eyes quickly followed the twisting rope to a vent in the ceiling. Steiner's shoe met his nose this time. He heard it pop and saw flashes of purple. Heard Lora savagely slapping at Chambers, saying, "No, no, no." Chambers laughing—lecherous and guttural. Myron threw himself toward the open window.

"Crazy fucker's trying to go out!" Steiner shouted. He sounded terrified or ecstatic.

Myron thought maybe the vent gave a little bit. He timed his next push for when Steiner came at him with the shoe again. It met him on the ear with a buzzing roar and he threw himself out the window, felt the air kiss his sweaty skin, heard a crumbling and a clanking and started his descent.

On the way down, he tried to think about nothing at all.

10.

He hit the cement and everything fractured and exploded before it imploded upon itself. He felt twisted up and inside out but surprisingly whole. He opened his eyes to stare up at a black sky streaked with lightning and pissing down rain.

*If you ask the Baron to cause the death of another, you be prepared to pay. But just know—he is the master of death and it's only he can take you there. So you make sure to pray for him to keep your heart beating and leave him out of that other man's business. That other man's for human hands. You and me and everyone else.*

Myron took a breath of the soggy air and felt his heart pound into life.

How many times would he be able to defy death?

He stood up, expecting to see a crowd of gawkers.

He didn't.

## 11.

What he saw—what he *could* see—was much worse. This was the world of his vision. This was the world Mama Hodap had shown him. This was not the world he had left behind. Only maybe it was that world, perverted and decayed.

This was still Wall Street. The buildings were still there but they were in shambles, crumbling ruins. Every building except for the Chambers Building. If anything, it was even taller than before and now it looked more like a tower than a building. For a moment, Myron thought it was glowing. Several torches were stood up along the side of the road, almost like primitive streetlamps, their flames guttering against the rain. Naked corpses were stacked on the sidewalks to either side of the road. Men, women, children, animals. All stripped and thrown there like garbage, in various states of decay. Now was not the time to mourn them. He had other things to do. He had a purpose and now that purpose was renewed. Mama Hodap had felt it when she had touched him. She had said he was the one. She had said he had been brought to her. He had been chosen. He had not found them. They had found him. For the first time since entering the sewers, he was able to understand what she meant.

He didn't put himself together and stand up after falling forty-three floors for nothing.

He tried to shake the vision from his head. It didn't do any good. It was no longer just a vision. It was very real, slouching in front of him. The torches still burned. The bodies were still there. The rain continued to pour. Lightning continued to flash. He was in the belly of chaos. He was in the middle of Wall Street, adjusted to fit this savage world.

He turned toward the Chambers building.

This time he was going to enter through the front door.

He had encountered Chambers. He was still alive. He still had his dignity. He was still an under man, still a resident down there at the bottom of the world. But he was not unequal. He knew that now.

As he drew closer to the building he saw that it wasn't made of brick and concrete like most buildings. Not anymore. Bones—gray, white, and black—made up the intricate framework. It was covered in a luminous membrane. The glowing, oozing tower contrasted against the black sky. He reached out to grab what may have been a handle or maybe just a jaw bone when the door opened to receive him.

He passed through it into the cramped, humid lobby.

12.

The door shut behind him and Myron knew he wouldn't be going back out that way even if he wanted to. He turned to survey the lobby area. It was arranged much the same as the old lobby area. The receptionist's desk was made up of various bones. These bones, enmeshed with the membrane and bone meal, made up the interior walls, as well. They made him think of fossils covered in semen. The membrane coated everything with that glow. It *had* to be glowing. He didn't see any other sources of light. The floor was some kind of black dirt or more bone meal. Maybe the ashes of the dead.

In front of him, the floor was moving, opening up.

He stood rooted in place, staring at the disturbance.

A pair of little hands reached up through the ashy floor, followed by a mostly familiar face.

Joanie.

He breathed the name aloud. "*Joanie*."

This was Joanie after death. Gray and rotten but still mostly intact. She hadn't really been dead very long. He reached out to help pull her from the ground. He took her hand and pulled gently. He could feel the bone separating from the joint and shuddered with the thought of the arm coming off in his hand. He released her.

"Joanie," he said again.

"Daddy." Her vocal cords didn't work very well. The muscles of her mouth were mostly rotten. Dirt and insects filled her throat. It didn't sound like Joanie at all.

She pulled herself the rest of the way out. Black dirt caked her deteriorated clothes. He wanted to hug her but fought the urge. What good would it do? This wasn't his Joanie. He knew that. It would be impossible for his Joanie to be here. He imagined hugging her and having her fall to pieces in his arms just like she had died under his watch. He fought the crippling wave of grief and guilt threatening to pull him down.

"Follow me," Joanie said.

She turned to his left, walking with a quick, jerking shamble. She disappeared through a man-size opening shaped like a vagina. He followed her, pushing the thickly dripping membrane aside, the thick lips of the vagina painting him in the substance.

Once through the opening, he found himself in a claustrophobic chamber even more sickeningly humid than the lobby. It breathed around him. Slowly. A sleep breath.

"Joanie?"

"Up here, Daddy!"

He looked up. A deep shaft ascended up through the building. Perhaps this was the elevator at one point. It didn't make any sense. The shaft was lined with what looked like circular bones, monstrous ribcages. He grabbed the first rung and began climbing.

His new body felt strong and powerful. Up to the task or merely equipped to take him to some awful end.

He knew where he was going.

All the way to the top.

Somewhere along the way, he lost sight of Joanie. But he figured he didn't lose sight of her. She was probably never there in the first place.

He climbed the rungs smoothly and as quickly as he could.

The shaft continued to ooze and breathe around him.

# MARKET ADJUSTMENT

On the way, he thought about the path that had brought him here.

13.

Shortly after the death of his family, Myron turned his back on the homeless shelters and the free government care that went along with them. As far as he was concerned, the only thing they had succeeded in doing was killing Melinda and Joanie. In the shelters and on the streets, he had heard whisperings of all kinds of things. It wouldn't do to go out looking for a job because a storm was brewing and the factories weren't hiring anyone and would probably be shutting down shortly. You could move out west but work was just as scarce out there and they paid slave wages for brutal days of backbreaking labor. None of that mattered to Myron. With his family gone, he didn't have anyone to work for anyway.

But Myron had kept his ears open. Eventually, rooting through a trash can behind a diner in Hell's Kitchen, he found Kevin Pierce. Pierce told him about a group of people who lived in the sewers and the subways. The Enclave, Pierce called them. Myron spent the day with Pierce. He was hungry and dirty just like everyone he knew. But he seemed calm. Toward the end of the day, Myron thought he had it figured out.

"You ain't searchin," he said to Pierce.

"Whaddya mean?"

"Well, ever'body else's lost ever'thin but they're tryin to get it back. They're all bunched up and anxious."

Pierce threw back his head and laughed, scratching the thick beard on his neck.

Then he told Myron about the Enclave.

And Mama Hodap.

Myron, who didn't have anything else to search for, followed Pierce down.

So Myron went below and embraced what he knew he had always been. An under man.

He was introduced to Mama Hodap and she told him what he needed to do. He didn't disagree with her.

She was the closest thing the Enclave had to a spiritual leader. Or any kind of leader. She took him to that disused utility room. She filled it with incense smoke and laughter and a sense of life Myron hadn't felt in a very long time. Meeting her for the first time, he had been nervous. All the nervousness melted away when he looked into her soulful eyes and felt her calming touch. She had told him how he could be one of them.

*You gotta contribute fore you can partake.*

And she had told him what he needed to do. He was skeptical at first. He no longer took anything at face value.

She had given him a vision and the vision had become a kind of truth in his heart and he hadn't doubted her since.

Even now, climbing up this abstract elevator shaft, climbing to a fate that might very well be his death, he didn't doubt Mama Hodap. She spoke from an under place and that place held a lot more truth than the offices situated quietly in the tops of skyscrapers.

14.

He reached the top of the membranous shaft and crawled out. He hadn't noticed any other openings along the way. It was designed to take him to this place. It was designed to take all visitors to this place.

But what was this place?

He emerged into a low, narrow hallway. He stayed on his hands and knees. There wasn't any room for him to stand. There were no windows in this nightmare hallway. The only light came from the glow of that mucous substance. Toward the end of the hallway, he searched for an entrance to Chambers. He saw something that

*32*

looked like an anus at the far end. That was probably it. He crawled along thinking he should be exhausted after his climb but he wasn't. He still felt strong. He still felt powerful and he wondered if this was from the gods Mama Hodap had equipped him with or if it was from the woman herself. Or maybe it was something that came from inside him. Maybe his instinct for revenge and survival was stronger than he had given himself credit for.

Drawing closer to the anus door, he noticed the awful stench seeping from it. It wasn't completely unexpected. When he thought of sliding through it, he gagged. He raised himself into a crouch and placed his hands palms together before inserting them into the center of the anus. He took a deep breath, closed his eyes and sprang forward, hoping the sphincter wouldn't constrict and trap him.

Finally thankful for the membrane coating him, he slid through effortlessly and ended up in a warped version of the previous Chambers reception area.

The same woman was still strapped to the receptionist desk.

Her skin was now a ghostly gray. Her clothes had been stripped off. Her sizable breasts fell to her sides. The ax he had used to chop down the door was stuck into her chest. Her dead eyes were frozen wide open with terror and a black tongue lolled from her mouth. Her legs were spread wide, dried blood crusting her sex. Myron's stomach sank. It was the ax. He felt partly responsible for this. But he wasn't the one who held the ax. He wasn't the one who had plunged it down into the innocent's chest.

Chambers was.

Would he still be in his office?

He turned to face the door, ready to make his final drive.

It wasn't going to be that easy.

The door was guarded. Two men, maybe Steiner and Todd, with the heads of the dogs, watched Myron. The one on the left growled at him. The one on the right dropped to his hands and knees, his lean thigh muscles flexing.

*Papa Legba opens doors for you.*

Mama Hodap's words came back to him but he still didn't want to invoke the god to get through this door. He couldn't help but think she had some other door in mind. This was still just a physical door and he had rapidly come to learn that all physical doors are made to be kicked down. He sidestepped quickly to his right and wrapped his hand around the grip of the ax. He yanked hard but it was firmly planted in the woman's chest. He grunted and yanked again as the first dogman pounced on him, knocking him back onto the floor and clamping his teeth to his neck. His hand groped for the ax but found only air.

The dog certainly had the killer instinct.

And Myron should be on his way to death right now but knew he wasn't. He'd made the offering to the Baron. Even better than a regular offering, it was a blood offering, however inadvertently that had been.

So let the blood flow.

Let the bullets fly.

Let the knives plunge and the teeth gnash.

With the dogman's jaws still clamped to his neck, its head jerking back and forth to rend the wounds even wider, Myron rolled over onto the dogman. He clamped the jaws shut with his hands, squeezing with his new strength. He could feel the blood pumping out of his neck. It was blood he didn't need. Not here, anyway. Until Papa decided to swing open death's black door, Myron wasn't going.

The dogman kicked beneath him, Myron's blood filling its mouth.

He thought about the stock certificates being shoved down his throat and clamped the dogman's jaws shut even harder. It gagged and tried to spit beneath him. Blood frothed out of its nostrils.

Myron wondered why the other dogman hadn't attacked him from behind. Maybe it was afraid. Maybe it didn't care. If they were Todd and Steiner, Myron figured they had been vicious backstabbers in the real world and didn't know why they would be any less so here.

The dogman stopped twitching beneath Myron. Its eyes rolled back in its head.

When Myron stood up, he found out where the other dogman had gone. It was sniffing the crotch of the sacrificed woman. Even if it was part man, it still had the brain of a dog.

Good boy, Myron thought, as he finally managed to work the ax out of the woman's chest.

"Stay," he said, and barely managed to suppress a laugh.

The dogman continued to lick at the blood caked between the woman's legs.

Myron raised the ax back over his head. He brought it down as hard as he could. The dogman had a thick neck. The ax severed the half closest to Myron. A torrent of blood sprayed out over the woman, some clinging to her pallid skin, some dripping down the strange bone desk.

15.

It wasn't a door guarding him from Chambers' office so much as more membrane. Thick and oozing from the boned frame. Myron clutched the ax tightly and stepped through the opening. The membrane stuck to his skin. He walked slowly into the center of the breathing room. The sensation was almost like being on a boat, rocking back and forth in gentle waves.

The room glowed brightly. It was strewn with cash, gold, stock certificates, and currencies from around the world. He almost didn't see Chambers sitting on something resembling a throne made from bones roughly where his desk used to be.

Like in a dream, the thing sitting there looked nothing like Chambers, but Myron knew it had to be. He was naked. His skin stretched tightly over his skeleton, pale white but gorged with blood, giving him an almost rosy complexion. Dark red nails grew from his hands and feet. A sickly smooth pouch replaced his genitals. His eyes were small and black.

And, it took Myron a moment to realize it, but Chambers was pulsing, his whole body expanding and contracting with the rhythm of a heartbeat.

Thud. Thud. Thud.

Myron almost wanted to touch him just to make sure he wasn't imagining it.

"What are you doing?" Chambers voice sounded like sandpaper gargling blood, but with the same gruff cadence it had before.

Myron thought about charging him with the ax, chopping him up until there was nothing.

But he couldn't move. He was rooted in place. The membrane had thickened and become like a rope, clinging to his clothes, reaching into his clothes and adhering to his skin.

"You know what I'm doin," Myron said. He felt stupid opening his mouth around this man. He felt small. Poor. Dumb. Uneducated. But he knew none of those things made him any less than this man.

Chambers chuffed out a laugh.

"I know what you're *trying* to do but let me assure you: Many have tried and many have failed. You don't know what you're up against."

"I have a pretty good idea."

"Is that so? Let's hear it."

"A monster."

He coughed out a laugh again. "You wish it was that easy. You're a simpleton. You don't know what it's like to become."

"Become what? A monster?"

"A god."

"You're hardly a god."

"You're right. I can only aspire. But the gods will continue to give me power if I continue to serve them."

"I don't serve gods. Any gods."

"Well, then you are even simpler than I thought. You're used to the gods of civilization." Chambers picked up some coins to his right and let them plink back down into the pile. "The gods of this. That's what makes you so civilized. The gods you've known don't know the meaning of chaos and survival within that chaos. The gods of civilization were made to be housed by churches and books. They are gods of convenience, there to serve the believer when convenient. It makes it easy to deny their existence. I haven't seen any proof myself. But my gods are the old gods. The oldest gods in the cosmos. And getting some of their power is as close as any one of us will ever get to them."

"The only god you serve is greed."

"Greed? Greed for what."

"Money."

"Money? Hardly. Although my gods did create money. In order to collapse a civilization, you have to give it the tools to build itself so that people can forget about the old ways. So people can forget what it's like to live in fear. Fear of their neighbor. Fear of the creatures in the night. Fear of starvation. You have built walls between yourselves and fear. And you let us build these altars to the gods. Our gods. And we found a way to turn currency into souls. We found out how to deaden them, eat them. And with each soul death, we move a little deeper into your world. And people like me, we are the hearts in these altars, moving the blood of our gods from hand to hand and taking it back and hoarding it when we need to. Tell me, Mr. Barnes, how's your soul doing? Bet you still wish Joanie and what's her face were around. Don't be surprised I know all this about you. I knew when you called. I knew how you pleaded with the clerks. But none of that helped. It amused me, sure. I don't know how many laughs you gave me. You lost your job. You lost your money. You lost your house. You lost your family. I can see inside of you. I can see how small you are inside. Now you're just a pawn in someone else's game and you're trying to turn it into something more than it is. I think you got back to the fear. Might have even found some gods of your own, despite what you said."

"It's so much more than that."

"Is it?"

Myron felt the membrane separate into something like tentacles, reaching up through his shirt and coiling around his neck, around the wound from the dogman. Myron felt no pain.

"Let's be honest, Mr. Barnes. You've said you don't serve gods so the only things you have left are life and death. You're alive, playing the game, being a pawn for some nigger who lives in the sewer, or you can die and hope there is some afterlife to reunite you with your family. Or…"

"Or what?"

"Or you can follow me through this door." Chambers motioned to the door behind him. It was the same door Myron had seen back in the real world, looking strangely anomalous amidst the bones and ooze. He'd wondered what was behind it then and he still wondered.

"What's behind the door?"

"Behind the door is the world you left behind. So you can go back to that world and I can make you a very rich man. All that worrying about money you've done over the course of your life would be over. You can start a new family. You can still remember your old family, but you'll have to start this new family just to show them how well you can provide for them. And I could give you the means to provide for them. You would have everything you need. You could give them everything they need. Your sense of worth would finally be restored."

"In return for what?"

"Nothing at all. You will, of course, be serving my gods, but you already said you do not have faith in your gods so, really, what difference does it make?"

"All the difference in the world." Myron raised the ax.

"You don't want to do that."

But he did want to do it. He could stand here and listen to Chambers talk for hours. Promise him things. That was how Chambers had gotten where he was today. Talking. Promises. Getting people to do things for him and offering what in return? Money? For what Chambers was asking for, money seemed a poor compensation.

Myron hoisted the ax above his head and threw it with everything he had before the membranous tentacles could wrap around his arms and restrain him. It sailed toward the pulsing heart of the old gods.

The ax struck Chambers in the shoulder and blood exploded outward. More blood than could possibly have been inside him. It spewed out in a slowly dying fount, covering the room, covering Myron.

The floor tilted beneath Myron. He thought about all those collapsed buildings around it and wondered if this one was collapsing too. Or maybe it was some kind of freakish earthquake.

The building lurched to the other side.

A deafening sound rumbled through the building, up behind the walls.

He reached down to begin tearing the tentacles away. Wrapping his hands around their slimy surface, he could feel the same breathing sensation he had felt since entering the place.

The breaths were further apart than previously.

He continued tearing at the tentacles, not knowing what he would do once he was free.

The building lurched again.

16.

The building was moving. Myron had to find a way out.

With each lurch, the treasure in Chambers' office jostled around. The paper currency stuck to the membrane and blood while the coins and the gold clattered together with a happy jingle. The thickening membrane moved over Chambers, pulling him against the wall, cocooning him. The ax still jutted from his shoulder. The building moved with a slow gait. Myron wished there were windows. He wanted to see the absurd spectacle of this building lumbering down Wall Street, in between the crumbling ruins, trodding on the piles of dead bodies.

He pulled the last coil of membrane from around his ankle.

He moved toward Chambers. He pulled the ax from him. He looked at the heavy door set into the bones and the ooze. He wanted to open it. He wanted to see what was behind it. Would there be some kind of answer or just more nothing?

Myron chopped Chambers free from his cocoon.

He felt the building lift. The trotting gait no longer disrupted the office. Now he had a plunging feeling in his stomach and a feeling of weightlessness.

Was the building flying?

He slung Chambers over his shoulder.

Again he looked at the door. He turned the handle but it wouldn't budge. It didn't turn at all. Myron wondered if the handle was even real. He thrust Chambers up higher on his shoulder so he could hold the ax with both hands. He drew it back and slammed it against the door even though he wasn't sure it was made of wood. Wasn't sure the ax would do any good.

It didn't.

The ax shattered—metal and wood—and it felt like Myron's hands shattered along with it. Deep vibrations rattled through his bones, reaching all the way back to his spine.

He would have to take his chances.

If this wasn't the door Papa Legba was supposed to open then maybe he was making a horrible mistake. But he didn't have any other choices.

He invoked the image of Papa Legba standing by the door. The deity looked at him as if to ask if he was sure this was what he wanted.

Myron nodded.

The door opened.

## 17.

What he saw beyond was swirling blackness. A dark night over New York or this other world he had fallen into. He walked to the edge of the door. The building was flying. Black water churned below him. The building had been flying but now it seemed to be descending. Chambers had said the building was an altar but could he have been wrong? Could he have been lying? Could the building have been the old god? Could Chambers have been the heart of the old god? And now the old god was trying to go home, to the depths of the ocean, back to some pre-civilization where chaos was the norm?

There were too many questions for Myron.

Perhaps he would ask Mama Hodap about them some other time.

For now, he had to get out of the building. Away from this dying god. He had to go through the door.

He clutched Chambers tightly and leapt through the door.

He felt himself falling rapidly through the rain, felt the water sting his face, saw lightning flash around him.

He closed his eyes and opened them back in Chambers' real office. The one in the Chambers building at the corner of William and Wall.

In one hand he held an ax. In the other hand, he held a black, meaty heart.

The office was still in relative disarray. Blood was everywhere. Todd and Steiner lay on the floor, sprawled out and mauled. A dog sat above each one of them. Both the dogs looked content, panting happily. They made no move to attack Myron.

Money, shit, and stock certificates were mixed in with the blood.

The smell was ferociously terrible.

Chambers' desk had been uprighted. Chambers lay on the surface, naked, the flesh of his torso ripped open to hang in flaps on either side of him.

Myron grabbed a wad of the stock certificates and wrapped them around the heart and put it in the pocket of his worn coat. He wiped his hands on some hundred dollar bills and let them flutter back down to the floor. Myron left the office and wondered what the police would make of this when they came upon it.

The receptionist area was relatively clean.

He wondered if the sacrifice had been claimed as brutally as she had been in that other world or if she had managed to escape. Had Lora managed to escape?

These were things he would happily put behind him.

He took the service elevator down to the lobby and slinked out the service exit like the under man he was proud to be. He was going back to the bottom. Back below, and he was taking a little piece of this place with him.

Disorientation dizzied him as he stepped back out onto Wall Street.

The furor and chaos had died down.

Most of the brokers had probably gone home.

The whole area felt decompressed.

The streets and sidewalks were wet with rain and there was a chill in the air. He breathed deeply.

"Hey, buddy, ya got my money?"

The hotdog vendor was pushing his cart along the sidewalk. Packing it in for the evening.

"I said I'd pay ya back."

"Hey, buddy, I was just givin ya a hard time. One hotdog ain't gonna kill me, right?"

Myron reached into his pocket and pulled out the two hundred dollars.

"Look, mister, you ain't gotta…"

Myron handed him one of the bills.

"I can't take this, mister."

"I insist. You… performed an invaluable service. Besides, I still have another one right here, huh? Hey, between you and me—this is free money."

"You steal it?"

"I *look* like a thief?"

"Nah, you look honest."

"Take it and do somethin nice for your wife and kids."

The vendor looked down at the bill and shook his head. "It's been a weird goddamn day."

"For you and me both."

The vendor slipped the bill into his pocket and glanced around suspiciously like he was guilty for having this much money handed to him at once.

"You have a real good evening, mister." The vendor went back to pushing his cart.

Myron turned and walked in the opposite direction, flipping a dismissive wave behind him.

He hailed a cab. He slid into the back. The cabbie was listening to the radio. The market had finished down for the day. Tough economic times were coming, all the experts agreed.

Myron sighed with relief. It felt like all of his tough times were coming to an end.


18.


Later, in the sewer beneath Harlem, after leaving the cabbie with the remaining hundred dollar bill, Myron watched Mama Hodap's face light up as he presented her with the heart. The other members of the Enclave seemed ecstatic as well. It was a small victory. One they celebrated by roasting the heart over a pitiful fire and dividing it equally before eating.

There were still people like Chambers out there.

Still people who served the old gods.

The news spoke of a collapse and Myron knew this meant the hearts of Wall Street might lie low for a year or two years or maybe even more, if they were really serious about it. But they would be back. They would make another move to stake a claim on the modern world. And Myron and Mama Hodap and the rest of the Enclave would be there to try and stop them.

# THE DUST SEASON

The caravan moved from east to west. One of the last genuine freak shows, the campers and trucks rattled through the dust. That was about the only thing Bradley could remember. The dust. It felt like they were following some eternal drought across the continent. Everywhere, there was dust.

Through the bars of his trailer, at a gas station, Bradley watched the feet shift through the film. He couldn't bring himself to raise his head and look at the faces that belonged to those shuffling feet. The faces seemed too sad. This was the bad time of year when the dust mixed with the humidity and formed some kind of airborne mud that filled the lungs. But, even though it was everywhere, the dust was the least of Bradley's worries.

Something terrible had happened.

Flashes of it came to him, as flitting as his geological location. He went to sleep thinking Georgia, Georgia, Georgia, we're in Georgia and it would be Mississippi when he came to. And with the waking, there was the surging electric blue pain, an afterimage left like a tear soaked postcard in his memory.

It's a job, he told himself. Just like any other job. Think of it as a demotion, that's all.

No. No. It was more than that. Although he had no idea in what capacity, what area he had worked in before, he was well aware of who he was now.

The attractions had their own separate booths, small places made hastily from garish, crudely painted plywood and pressed board. Nowhere near as alluring as the banners that adorned the outside of the tent. Bradley's booth stank. It smelled like raw sewage, mildew, and rotting meat.

Helton was about ready to let the first group in. The grating sound of Helton's voice as he shouted promises at the undoubtedly small crowd sent more memories shredding through Bradley.

Helton—the tiny, hideous leader. Substantially under five feet tall, with pale skin that looked like it had been painted on with a sponge, Bradley knew Helton had something to do with his demotion.

Bradley cringed. Helton's voice, augmented through a cheap megaphone, made his insides squirm.

"Ladies and gentleman! Prepare yourselves for spectacles that can't be seen anywhere else. No sir. Rest assured that this is the only place where you will see a real, live giant. That's right, he stands through these doors, waiting to meet your gaze. But it gets stranger than that. Mr. Magneto will show you how he can hang from a steel beam with nothing but the magnetic force of his skin. We have a man with gills. A man who can lift barbells with his tongue. And tonight, making her first appearance—the Painted Lady! Watch her get another flesh piercing tattoo right in front of your very eyes…"

More memories. More excruciating than the first ones. Longer in length.

The Painted Lady hadn't always been the Painted Lady. She used to be Elastica, Queen of Bending. Unlike a lot of the other freaks, being the Queen of Bending didn't involve any physical deformity or mutilation. Bradley knew her as Eliza, the Hideous Leader's wife. But Bradley didn't let that stop him. When Eliza beckoned, Bradley answered. Each time they met, whether they slept together or not, was heaven for Bradley—

*He remembered now. He'd been the psychic, more of a money-raiser than a freakish attraction*

—and there were occasions when he really did have the gift. That was one of the reasons he enjoyed being with Eliza, her mind was so open and easy to enter. He stared into her eyes, crawled into her mind, and started opening doors. He felt like they had created a dark and secret world between them. They talked about running away. When we get to California, they agreed. Before the sideshow doubled back.

They were in this mental dreamland, hiding in the blackly magical woods of Louisiana behind that night's encampment. Before either of them could run off, the Hideous Leader, Strong Arm, and The Lift were upon them.

Helton's small white hands glowed in the dark and gripped Bradley's wrist, squeezing impossibly tight.

Strong Arm guffawed. "We thought you'd see us comin, future boy."

They were both dragged out into the pool of light created by the circle of campers and trucks. The other freaks wandered out of their temporary homes, the only ones they knew. It was rare that they got to watch a show themselves.

Between the three of them, they had Eliza stripped bare in no time. She tried to struggle, tried to fall down, but they kept standing her upright. Mr. Fish, the man with gills, doubled as the resident tattoo artist. At that hour, he was a very drunk tattoo artist. The Hideous Leader shaved Eliza's head and pubis, savagely dragging the razor along until too much hair got caught up in it. Then he simply rubbed the blade against the moist grass and went back to work. Eliza screamed when the needle went in at her crown. Helton barked around his cigar, "Go deep with em. We don't want none of em wearin off."

Eliza continued to scream. It wasn't long before other onlookers were invited to join in the tattooing. A few of the men squabbled over her breasts and between her legs. Every few minutes, the Hideous Leader threw a bucket of cold water on Eliza to rinse the blood away and keep her in a state of semi-consciousness.

Bradley had stayed tapped into her secret place during the whole ordeal. What he saw, he guessed, was Eliza's life flashing before her eyes. All of that hitting him at once was overwhelming. And over top of that, like a burning blanket, was the pain. Although her skin went numb to the physical pain relatively quickly, the mental anguish was soul draining and constant.

Bradley's memory faded out as his mind had wanted to that night.

The Hideous Leader droned on: "That's right. Just last week, she was the Human Scab, but here she is in her full, multicolored regalia. But that's not all—the Strongest Man in the World, Siamese Twins, the *real* Elephant Man and, this one, folks… this one I'm gonna bring out first… Now, it's kind of an experiment so I want you to make him feel really welcome. Ladies and gentlemen—I give you the Quarter Man."

The yellow bug-swamped light hit Bradley. He swooned, stuck out his arms to brace himself from the fall and—

When they were finished with Eliza they took her out and threw her into the dust. Bradley quickly learned what they meant to do with him. Struggle was useless. His breath came in harsh, ragged bursts. They threw him to the ground and tied his wrists and ankles to tent stakes. The Hideous Leader made sure to sharpen the knives by his ear, digging his little knees into Bradley's back. Helton started on his backside, just below the buttocks, and removed each of Bradley's legs. Mercifully, he was unconscious when they cauterized the wounds, despite the Hideous Leader's attempts to revive him.

—and realized that there was no fall to brace. His hands were now his feet. His feet and legs were somewhere else altogether.

# THE DUST SEASON

He looked out at those blank faces, wondering how he was still alive. Not for long, he thought. He could feel and smell the blackish-yellow tentacles of infection, working their way up his spinal column.

And from another booth came faint glimpses of the secret place, ruinous now, so much gray dust, filled with a sense of dread. When they covered her body with tattoos, they made sure to leave a few blank spaces. Tonight, the first one would be filled. By the time they got to the last one, the freak show would need another quarter man or, perhaps, a quarter woman.

# THE MAN WITH THE FACE LIKE A BRUISE

"Eli," she whispered into his ear.

Nothing.

She shifted in the bed, turning over to face him.

"Elijah?"

He only whimpered and turned away from her. She leaned her head over top of his, feeling the heat coming off his face. She pushed her lips into the stubble that grew from his jaw line, sliding her tongue between her lips, pressing it against the stubble, running it up the sleep greasy sheen of his cheek until she could taste the tear that had trickled from one of his closed eyes.

"Eli?" she whispered again.

Still nothing.

She rolled back over, pulled the sheet up to her chin, and closed her eyes against the dawn.

After the blueness had left the room, replaced with a yellow that was harsher and fuller of sun, Eli woke up. Maya was lying next to him, already awake. He reached over, beneath the sheet, pulled down a little lower now, and ran his hand up her silk smooth thigh.

"Morning, sweetness," he mumbled through drymouth.

"You were whimpering again." She didn't even look at him, just kept staring up at the ceiling.

"Was I?"

"Actually crying this time."

"Did I wake you?"

"No, I was already awake."

He rolled over and nibbled her ear.

"Look, Eli, is there something you need to tell me?"

"About what?"

"It's not like you, that's all. The whimpering. The crying. I want you to tell me what the hell's the matter with you."

Eli leaned across the bed, over Maya and her fabulous heat, to grab his cigarettes and lighter from the nightstand. He brought himself back over to his side and propped the pillow up against the headboard, shook out a cigarette and lit it. Through the thin, twirling veil of gray smoke, he looked at their small apartment. They had something good. He liked what they had created over the past year. They never argued. They didn't really have any worries and, until this past month or so, they had had some really great sex. Eli didn't want to lose any of that.

Maya sighed into the heavy yellowness of the room.

"Are you going to tell me?" she said.

Eli took another drag and crushed the cigarette out.

"Yeah, I'll tell you."

Sometimes, when everything was blue, Elijah didn't just see what was in front of him. There was something else. It was like the air around him was too thin or something. Almost like he could see through it. And it wasn't just his sight that was affected. He heard things too, when everything was blue.

It started right before Eileen and Cynthia died. The week before, to be exact. June 15. More than two years ago. Two years and one week ago.

Dawn in the bedroom of their new house in the suburbs and

# THE MAN WITH THE FACE LIKE A BRUISE

Elijah had woken up and looked around the room. The blue filled the room and inside the blue, Elijah saw the swirling shapes. He got out of bed and walked into the middle of the room, deeper into the blue, Eileen sleeping soundly, Cynthia still tucked away in her room with the Dr. Seuss murals painted on the walls.

The blue wasn't like any other color Elijah had ever seen. It almost seemed like calling it blue was to do it some sort of injustice. It couldn't be categorized like that. It was the blue of a hundred different skies. The blue of Heaven, perhaps.

Elijah stood in the middle of the room, shivering cold and still sweaty—clammy. He felt the blue moving all around him. He felt it brush up against his ear and whisper something no more intelligible than the wind. Sitting down, he marveled at the way the blue could coil itself up before slowly, hypnotically unfurling. He admired the color and the sheer mystery of it.

Over the next week, his feelings changed.

The blue continued to visit him, gaining in intensity.

Three days after the first, Elijah noticed there were people in the blue. Spirits maybe. Ghosts. Who knew? He wasn't sure he *wanted* to know. By the end of that fourth day, he could make out some of the faces in the blue. There must have been hundreds. All surfacing through the blue before receding.

Before the sun ate the blue that day, he saw the face like a bruise. That was when he knew everything wasn't going to be okay.

On the fifth day, there were fewer faces.

On the sixth day, even fewer.

On the seventh day, the day of Eileen and Cynthia's death, the only face remaining was the one that looked like a bruise. That was when Elijah assumed the man with the face like a bruise had somehow consumed the other faces. Maybe he would have opened it up to speculation, something to ponder, to think about, maybe even ask somebody about, if it weren't for the car crash that took Eileen and Cynthia that night.

The grief in and of itself was crippling and then there were all the legal ramifications on top of that, the people in suits telling him his time for grieving was over, and the blue was gone anyway so there wasn't really anything to think about.

A little more than a year later he met Maya and his grief was replaced with love. Although the love was somewhat tainted with guilt. So much guilt, in fact, that Elijah could never really bring himself to tell Maya about the previous loves of his life. Initially, he told himself he was just waiting for the right time. Eventually, he convinced himself there wasn't a right time. He had waited too long. To tell her now would surely cost him the relationship.

But the blue had come back—and the man with the face like a bruise—and Maya had heard him crying and whimpering names, fragments. Enough to make her suspicious. That, on top of the impotence and the despondency, was sure to ruin everything he and Maya had.

Neither one of them had gotten out of bed to open the windows or turn on the air conditioner and Maya lay beside Elijah, the tears coming out of her eyes mingling with the sheen of sweat on her cheeks. She brushed the moisture off with the back of an already moist hand and reached over to the nightstand to get a cigarette. He had never seen her smoke. She seemed like a different woman as she greedily lit the cigarette. She inhaled the cigarette and coughed up a combination of tears, phlegm, and smoke. She sat up, keeping the sheet pulled to just above her breasts.

"I thought," she said, "that you had found someone else. I thought those were the names you were saying. Some whore at the office you were fucking."

"I would never do anything like that to you." He put his hand on her thigh, ran it up to the crease between where her leg met her pubis.

"I thought that was the whole reason why you couldn't... you know."

"I would never cheat on you. You know that... *don't* you?"

# THE MAN WITH THE FACE LIKE A BRUISE

She shook her head. "It happens."

There was a moment of awkward silence. Maya's crying increased. Unable to finish the cigarette, she crushed it out. Elijah moved his hand onto the soft mound of her sex. "It happens," she mumbled again through a thick mouth. He brushed his hand over her clitoris and then stopped, bringing his hand quickly away.

"I need to go," he said.

"Don't go," Maya cried.

"I have to work. I need to go."

He dressed in a hurry and left the apartment, slamming the door on his way out.

Once in the car, he knew he wasn't going to work. He was too angry. He didn't exactly know why. He sat in the hot car, sweat rolling down his face, shaking with anger. Slowly, he composed himself enough to pull away from the curb and take the twisted mess inside his head with him.

Stopping at the liquor store, he bought a bottle of Jim Beam and continued on to the Moston Memorial Gardens. There, he would be able to sit. To contemplate. Sort some things out.

He opened the Jim Beam as soon as he got out to the car and was nearly drunk by the time he got to the cemetery. He pulled the car up near Eileen and Cynthia's gravesites and stumbled across the freshly manicured lawn until he reached their tombstones. Once there, he sat down in between them, the bottle between his legs.

It was then he decided to sort some things out, to try and figure out why he was so goddamn enraged.

The most obvious fact was that this was the two-year anniversary of their deaths. The grief and anger had never really relented since he had received the call at home to come to the hospital and identify the bodies. The grief, he knew, would have to subside on its own. It would never go away completely. He didn't expect, didn't even really *want*, that to happen. The grief was like a memory. To remove the grief, he would have to take away all the memories of them. He didn't want that. Memories were the only things he had left.

The rage, though. That was something different altogether. It was something he hadn't expected and, once upon him, couldn't figure out how to get rid of. Entangling himself in hostile relationships with virtually everyone he knew didn't seem to do the trick. That merely rendered him isolated and friendless. It wasn't just the world he was mad at. It was Eileen, too. If she had been more alert, maybe, or a better driver, then none of it would have happened. He knew that was ludicrous, of course, but knowing it didn't stop the feelings and the thoughts rushing through his head. Knowing it almost made it worse, turning the whole situation into some all-consuming paradox.

God was at fault too, naturally. Elijah had never been a very religious person but he wouldn't have considered himself an atheist until that day. A god that would kill a beautiful, successful woman in the prime of her life and an innocent child wasn't a god worth believing in. A god that would force him to suffer as much as he had after their deaths was a god that was better off dead.

Completely drunk at this point and watching the thunderheads gather up their black dresses of grief and march toward the graveyard, he realized there was a new dimension to his anger and he finally figured it out.

Maya was cheating on him.

The signs were there, he had merely refused to acknowledge them. But now that he did, now that he told himself she was cheating on him, the pieces fell into place.

It started with the way she was acting this morning. How she had told him affairs happened. It wasn't even the way she said it, "It happens," it was the way she completely broke down after he had told her he wasn't cheating on her. Like, after her suspicions were denied, she was the guilty one. It would be completely like Maya to fuck someone to get even with him.

Then Elijah remembered something else. Actually, it was some*one* else. All last week, about the same time everything became blue again, Elijah had seen the same man coming from the direction of their apartment building. In a small town like Moston, it wasn't unusual to see the same faces over and over again, but he hadn't seen this man until last week and he never saw him at any other time.

Elijah remembered touching Maya this morning and how unresponsive she was.

Well, he thought. There's only one way to prove it.

With that, he stood up, guzzled down the rest of the bourbon, pulled some flowers away from a neighboring grave and put them into the empty bottle, setting it down in between the graves as a small reminder he was there.

On his way back into town he drove straight through the storm. By the time he reached the apartment the storm had subsided and the air around him resonated with the ozone blue of sun trying to break through dark clouds. He did the best parking job he could muster, nearly popping the tire as the car flew up onto the curb. It didn't matter. He didn't plan on being there for very long anyway.

He knew what he expected to find and, at this point, a scary thought, it was almost what he *wanted* to find. He wondered if they would actually be fucking or maybe Maya was now feeling guilty and blowing the guy off. Whoever the creep was, Elijah felt certain he would try and get a little something from her before saying his goodbye.

Elijah threw open the door from the street and bounded up the stairs.

Would they even bother locking the doors?

He had his key ready but, turning the knob, discovered he didn't even need it. Hell, the anticipation of getting caught had to be half the thrill of it.

One could not see the front door from the bed. It was one of the small touches that made the apartment feel a little less like an efficiency.

Elijah grabbed the aluminum Louisville Slugger he kept propped against the door in case of intruders. It had never really occurred to him before that was probably the worst place he could have kept it if anyone wanted to break in. It would be like arming the criminal. Of course, there was a gun in the bedside table. He anticipated Maya going for that if he didn't act quickly enough. Elijah hated guns. He had no intention of trying to go after it himself.

As he rounded the corner, his mind took a quick snapshot of what was happening on the bed before he moved in to put a stop to it.

Maya was lying back, her eyes closed, her ass supported by the edge of the bed. Her sundress was pushed up to her waist and there was a man's head between her legs, his hands wrapped around her hips, one of her legs thrown over his right shoulder.

Elijah moved in quickly, taking a firm grip on the bat's friction tape and hoisting it above his head. Maya must have heard him. She opened her mouth, trying to say something, but it wouldn't come out before the bat smashed across the man's upper back, the fat of it landing on his left shoulder, the very tip of it connecting with Maya's right leg.

The man let out a pitiful groan as he fell to the floor, struggling to turn over onto his back and identify his assailant. Elijah was on him, pressing the bat down against his throat so he couldn't yell. He needed this to be as subdued as possible because this wasn't the end. The more he thought about it, the more gruesome he wanted it to be.

"Everyone needs to shut the fuck up," Elijah said calmly. "If anyone decides to cry out or yell for help then I'm swinging the bat again. And this time I'll hit something more vital."

"Eli…" Maya said.

Elijah put more weight on the bat and watched the man's face turn purple.

"I think you should be quiet, Maya," he said. "Now, we're all going down to the car. If we pass anyone and you try and say something to them, I'll beat you both to death before any help can arrive. When we get down to the car, you are going to get in the driver's seat, Maya. Do you understand that?"

She nodded her head.

"Good," Elijah said. "Loverboy here is going to get in the passenger seat and I'm going to sit in back. We're driving to Keifer Road, where it meets Salton Lane. Do you know where that is, Maya?"

She nodded her head again. Her mouth was pulled tight and she was trembling, exactly what Elijah wanted to see. Her hands were gripped tight over her knee, already swollen and purple.

"Do you think you're going to have trouble walking?" Elijah asked her.

She nodded her head.

"If you fall down, then I'm taking this bat through loverboy's head, do you understand?"

She nodded.

"Are you going to fall down?"

She shook her head.

"Good. Let's go. Maya, you first. Loverboy second."

Elijah pulled the bat away from the guy's neck and stood up, backing away from the small battery scene. The man still had his shirt on but now the back of the shirt contained a lump that looked something like a football. He had absolutely no use of his left arm and Elijah found the way he had to struggle to stand up quite comical. He chuckled a little.

This was definitely the guy Elijah had seen on the street in front of their apartment. They must have had some way of seeing Elijah coming so they could get him out of there in time. For some reason, this infuriated Elijah even more. The fact Maya didn't feel the need to be even more discrete about her affair. The fact neighbors had to have seen this man come into the apartment, never at the same time as Elijah. Elijah wondered if any of the neighbors had heard them fucking, heard the headboard beating against the wall. Surely they must have.

Maya limped slowly to the door, bracing herself on whatever objects she could find along the wall. Elijah didn't enjoy watching her as much. It had never really been his intention to hurt Maya. When Elijah looked at the man he saw the man with the face like a bruise. Not really, only symbolically. Just as the man with the face like a bruise had somehow taken everyone he had loved away from him before, so this man had come along two years later and done the same. But the man with a face like a bruise was only a spirit, quite possibly a metaphysical hallucination, impossible to destroy. In this man, Maya's nameless lover, Elijah had a very palpable target for his revenge. Elijah reached out and jabbed the man's swollen shoulder with the end of the bat, watching the cords in the man's neck draw tight as he stifled a wince.

They made their way down to the car, Elijah standing outside until he saw that Maya and her lover were in their assigned positions. Still cautious, he slid into the back seat, maintaining a firm grip on the baseball bat. After sitting down, vigilantly leaning forward, there was an awkward pause in the rhythm.

"Start the car," he barked at Maya.

"I don't know if I can use the gas pedal," she said.

"You don't need your leg to use it, just your foot. Now start the fucking car."

She did as she was told. Music from the Birthday Party filled the car, Nick Cave's hooting and barking, along with the churning and screeching of the guitar, matching what Elijah felt in his head. Maya's hand instinctively reached out to turn the volume down until she thought better of it. Elijah realized he was still in control of the situation.

The storm had now passed completely and the late afternoon was sparkling and humid.

"Roll down your window!" Elijah shouted over the music.

Maya rolled down the window.

# THE MAN WITH THE FACE LIKE A BRUISE

She pulled away from the curb and started down the road, where Main Street turned into the Pike. From there they would hit Keifer and be just about where Elijah needed them to be.

Elijah sat in the back seat, studying them—the tense musculature of their necks, the way their shoulders seemed all drawn up. He basked in it. He basked in what he had planned, never once thinking anything would stop it from going off.

But he didn't want to end anything without getting some answers first. Eileen and Cynthia had taken the open book with them, leaving Elijah to write up his own conclusions and close the book. It was something he didn't ever think he would be capable of doing. Of course, with their situation he had no control over it. He had simply decided it was the man with the face like a bruise and had spent the next two years of his life searching that man out. He wasn't going to let that happen again. He had the man with the face like a bruise right here in front of him and he wasn't going to let him get away.

Elijah slid the bat in between the two front seats and started ramming the stereo violently until it cracked, splintered, and the music went away.

"So, Maya, you never properly introduced me to loverboy here. I mean, in a round about way, I guess we were quite intimate but, shucks, I don't even know his name."

"Hunter," she said.

"Last name?"

"Green."

"Hunter Green? Sounds like a fucking golf course. So, Maya, how old a man is Hunter?"

"Twenty-three."

"Oh. Robbing the cradle a bit? Well, that's all fine, I guess I'm pretty much past my prime anyway. By the way, how big is Hunter's cock, Maya?"

She was silent.

Elijah quickly flicked the barrel of the bat to his right, smacking

Hunter on the side of the head, just hard enough to stun him and make a satisfying sound.

"I never measured."

"But surely you have an idea. Erect? What, both hands plus the head? Then some, maybe…"

"Nine inches."

"Hunter, does Maya give good head? I mean, is it up to your standards? I always found it pretty good, except that she could never really go all the way with it. You know, she could never get it all the way in without gagging."

Hunter stared dazedly ahead. "She's good," he said through clenched teeth.

"That's pretty vague there, Hunter. I mean, if you're nine inches then you have something on me so I know she wasn't able to get it all the way in."

"She tried."

"Well, sometimes that's the best you can ask for, I guess. Did you like the taste of her pussy? I ask this because I noticed you kind of feasting on it when I came home today."

"Yes."

"On a scale of one to ten?"

"Eight."

"Have you tasted a lot of pussy?"

"A few."

"So have you ever tasted a ten?"

"Yes."

"Who was she?"

"Lorna Brett. My sophomore year."

"So you like the young pussy?"

"I guess."

"Maya, did you let him fuck you in the ass? Did you fuck her in the ass, Hunter?"

"Once."

"How was it?"

# THE MAN WITH THE FACE LIKE A BRUISE

"Good."

"Not great?"

"It was good."

"She never let me fuck her in the ass. Not that I really tried all that much but variety's the spice of life, you know. It would have been something different, in between all those affairs with girls from the office. Right, Maya?"

"I'm sorry." She was crying, wiping the tears from her eyes.

"Doesn't feel good to have your life, your *secret* life all exposed like this, does it? I mean, my secret life, hell, it only involved me but yours was a little, I don't know, des*truc*tive maybe. Is that the right word for it?"

No one answered Elijah, there were a few seconds of silence, the car flapping along the ill-maintained road.

"So, did you ever come in her face, Hunter?" Elijah quickly pointed off to his right and said, "You're about to miss the turn, hon." Maya whipped the car onto Salton Lane. Elijah lost his balance momentarily but quickly found it again. "Because, you know, I always kind of wanted to but I could never really muster up the courage to ask her. I guess it's just one of those things you either have to be asked to do or you just gotta do at the spur of the moment. So, what about it, Hunt?"

"No."

"Same reasons? I mean, you wanted to, right? When she's having an orgasm, you can't look at those perfect little lips and not have the thought of coming onto them cross your mind."

"Yes, I wanted to."

"Okay, slow down a little bit. Stop at this bend."

But she didn't stop at the bend. She didn't even make it to the bend. Just before the road broke swiftly to the left, Maya cut the wheel to her right and the car rolled off the road and into a ditch. She wasn't going very fast and there wasn't really any damage, but everyone in the car was thrown around.

Elijah could tell what her intention was. Her intention was to wreck the car in such a way that he would not be able to open his door. Instead, all the doors were free to be opened. The front of the car had merely run into some small trees at the edge of the woods. Before Elijah could get his bearings, Maya had already opened her door and took off limping into the woods on the other side of the road. But Maya wasn't really his main concern. Elijah's main concern was the man in the front seat struggling with his door, trying to assemble some kind of propulsive rhythm with the one side of his body that worked.

Elijah beat him out of the car, baseball bat in hand.

Hunter opened his door, oblivious to Elijah standing outside of the car, and slid his legs out until they found the ground. Elijah, looking at Hunter's stretched out legs, swung the heavy bat across the man's knees. He was pretty sure at least one of them shattered. Elijah swung the bat three more times, the sound of connection becoming a little pulpier with each swing. Once he was certain Hunter was no longer mobile, he grabbed him and dragged him outside of the car.

Elijah was pleased to see Hunter was now suffering from hysterics. With his good arm, the man groped for Elijah's pants leg.

"Please," he sobbed. "I'll do anything you want me to do. Just let me go. Please."

Elijah squatted down next to Hunter.

"There is something you could do for me."

"Anything." Tears streamed down Hunter's straining face.

"Okay. I want you to look at that big sycamore. You can see how large it is. How it sticks up a little bit higher than the rest of the trees. Do you see it over there?"

Hunter nodded his head.

"Two years ago. Two years ago today, actually, my wife was driving a car that smashed into that tree. My daughter was also in the car. Did you know that sometimes God kills people?"

Hunter nodded his head again.

"Have you ever lost somebody that you loved more than

anything?"

"My mother," Hunter blurted out, sticky spit stretching between his lips as he spoke.

"I'm sorry to hear that," Elijah said. "So what did she die of?"

"Cancer."

"Oh, so you knew she was going to die?"

Hunter nodded.

"Do you know what it's like to lose someone suddenly? You wake up one morning and you're this person and before you go to sleep that night, supposing you *can* actually go to sleep, you find out you're someone else entirely. And sometimes, you find you don't really like the person you've become."

Elijah paused, looking at the sycamore, how it seemed to stretch toward the road, looking for victims. Below him, Hunter continued to whimper.

"Do you believe in God?" Elijah asked him.

"Yes," Hunter said without delay.

"That's good," Elijah said. "Now I'm going to give you a reason why you really shouldn't."

Elijah stood back up and stooped into the car, leaning across the front seats to pluck the keys from the ignition. He walked up the small but steep slope of the ditch until he got to the trunk of the car. He put the key into the lock and pulled the trunk up. Looking at the assorted contents of the trunk, Elijah crazily thought all trunks must look like they belonged to a serial killer—ropes, tarps, a flashlight, the tire iron, the jack and other random debris, all of which could be construed as sinister.

He grabbed a few of the bungee cords, with each end being a steel s-shaped hook, a pair of pliers and a length of chain. He didn't even know why the chain was in there.

He carefully but quickly descended the slope until he reached Hunter.

"I thought you said you were going to let me go!" Hunter screamed.

Elijah furiously kicked at the man's head. "I never said any such thing."

As he went to Hunter's feet, the man thrashed around, screaming frantically, but it did no use. His legs were shattered and immovable from the knees down. Elijah took the bungee cords and wrapped them tightly around his legs, just below his swollen knees, taking the rope around and then through the circle created by doing that. He took the pliers and squeezed each of the s-hooks shut so they couldn't dislodge themselves from one another, leaving one of them open.

With the chain slung over his shoulder, he grabbed the cords like a handle and pulled Hunter behind him. Going up the slope was the roughest part and Hunter screamed exceptionally loudly as the asphalt scraped at his back when they reached the road.

Elijah remembered what the length of chain was from. It was from the dog he and Eileen and Cynthia had had. Before he sold the house and got rid of it. The dog's name was Night. The chain was used in the backyard, part of the dog's runner that gave him free range of the yard while still being restrained.

Hunter fingered the clamp at the end of the chain, opening it and closing it around the end link of the chain so that it made a giant loop. He was oblivious to Hunter's panicked screams. Or maybe the screams were fuel.

He eyed one of the sycamore's thick branches hanging low over the road. Elijah threw one half of the looped chain over the branch, bringing it down and through the other half he held in his hand. Releasing that end, he pulled on the other side until the chain was secure around the branch. The ellipse of the chain now dangled just above his head.

Elijah went back to Hunter and dragged him toward the branch. Hunter screamed and twisted, trying to get away from Elijah, his fingers clawing at the asphalt until the ends of them were turned into bloody rags.

Elijah hoisted him up from the bungee cord bundle around his knees and raised him above his head. He was glad Hunter was not a fat man. Hunter swung his one good arm fiercely, raising it up and ramming Elijah in the groin. Elijah winced and briefly let go of the cords, sending Hunter to the asphalt on the top of his head. Hunter tried to slither away in some kind of hideously modified army crawl. Elijah took a deep breath and kicked at Hunter's good elbow until his torso was flush against the asphalt.

Snatching the heavy pliers from his back pocket, Elijah brought them down continuously on Hunter's arm until he was pretty sure he wouldn't be able to move it anymore.

Elijah dragged Hunter back over to the tree, again hoisting him up, happy and disappointed at the same time that some of the fight seemed to have left Hunter. Elijah pulled Hunter up until his head was even with Elijah's knees and stuck the open s-hook through one of the links in the chain, fastening the hook shut with the pliers.

By that point, Hunter had stopped struggling. Suspended there, his eyes rolled back in his head, drool came out of his mouth, running over his cheeks and pooling in his eye sockets before melding with his sweat-matted hair. Elijah retreated to the car, shutting the trunk and the other doors before sliding into the driver's seat.

The car started without a problem. Elijah gunned the ignition until the tires found traction and allowed him to strainingly back out of the ditch. He continued to back the car up the road, to allow for acceleration. He checked the rearview mirror to make sure another car wasn't coming along to ruin everything.

Suddenly, his breathing got caught up in his throat. His stiff, adrenaline-filled body was reduced to a shivering mass.

His face.

His face was the color of a bruise, dark blue swirling into black.

He gunned the accelerator, ripping his eyes from the mirror and watching the speedometer as it climbed.

The car hit the swinging Hunter and continued off the other side of the road, into the woods, crashing into a number of the trees.

Elijah sat in the car, all too quiet after the deafening crash, listening to the hissing of the engine, the quiet tinkling of glass dripping from the windshield and onto the dash. He felt blood running down his face. There were many other parts of his body he couldn't feel at all.

Slowly, he slid out of the door, dragging a bloody arm across his face to stop the blood running into his eyes. Walking toward the road, he kept his eyes on Hunter. Or what was left of Hunter. The car had ripped him in half and what hung from the branch looked like a pair of pants spilling some type of intestinal gore. Below Hunter, the road was covered in a pool of dark blood.

Elijah stood there, not knowing what to do.

Something hit him in the head and knocked him to the ground.

He stared up at the darkening sky.

Then he saw Maya, standing over top of him.

She was crying. She held a large rock with two hands.

"My God, look at you," she said. "What's wrong with your face?"

"He found me, Maya."

"Who found you, Elijah?"

"*He* did."

"I never knew you were so fucking miserable."

"Sometimes it happens, Maya. It happens."

Elijah closed his eyes.

Maya sat down on his torso and looked at him, her tears dripping down onto his face like a bruise. She raised the rock up above her head and brought it down on that face until it went away, becoming something else.

# THE PHOTOGRAPHER

Verner stood on the balcony of his 23rd floor penthouse suite. The city, with all of her glittering lights, still seemed cold to him. Despite the warm breeze coming in off the Pacific, the city was still cold. Was the feeling one of physical cold or was it one of isolation? That wasn't a question Verner asked a lot. Truthfully, he didn't really give a damn. It didn't really matter the city held all the grandeur and mystery of a corpse laid out on an autopsy table. What mattered to Verner was the power he held over the city. Like the woman in the other room, the city was something he would demolish.

Only, the woman in the other room wasn't really a woman at all, was she? No, Verner admitted to himself, she was probably just a girl. He doubted if she was more than fifteen or sixteen. Didn't matter now, did it? His business with her was done. How many others like her had there been? Countless, like the cold cities he moved through. Countless. Worthless.

Verner pulled his silk robe around his freshly bathed body and lit a Dunhill. He sighed, blowing out a stream of smoke. Tomorrow, he had to go into the Santo Corporation and tell the company president which people to terminate. It would be roughly half the corporation. Santo was the largest employer in the city. The move would be devastating. Tomorrow, as he had been so many days in the past, Verner would be God. As mysterious as God, too. The people who would find themselves without a job would never see him, would never know his name.

Verner went back into the expansive penthouse, figuring he'd have a scotch before retiring for the evening. He reminded himself to call a cab for the mess in the bedroom before completely retiring. Bringing the cigarette up to his mouth, he noticed a speck of dried blood under his thumbnail. Must have missed it in the shower, he thought. He sat down on the couch and took the top off a large, ornate wooden box sitting slightly crooked on the glass coffee table. That's where he kept all the random things like fingernail clippers, lighters, batteries—all the stuff there wasn't much of another place to put. Instead of the miscellany he usually saw, there rested a letter-sized envelope.

That's odd, he thought. He couldn't quite remember tossing it in there. Before eagerly tearing into the envelope, he noticed it hadn't come through the postal network. No return address. No postmark. Maybe it was something he'd carried home from one of the corporations.

He took out the few small pictures and it all came back to him.


It must have been a little more than thirty years ago now. The air raid had flushed them out. Well, the air raid had dropped the bombs that flushed them out. Verner's decimated troop was so terrified they were simply mowing down anything in their way.

Verner wasn't terrified, though. Each night, he slept soundly, awaking in the morning with a feeling of exhilaration rushing through his veins. War was quite simply a game where the strongest, the most cunning, survived. Verner had no doubt he was the strongest, both mentally and physically. There was slow-witted Tibbs from Tennessee. Wallace from someplace like North Dakota who always thought a snake was going to slither up and bite him while he shat. Bergman from New Hampshire acted like he'd rather be in Canada or Mexico, anywhere but here. There were others. Verner hated them as much as he did the people on the other side. More, probably, since he had to listen to all of their idiotic little conversations that usually involved the girl back home. Verner wanted to tell them that girl was undoubtedly getting her brains fucked out by some guy who was just waiting for them to leave—in short, someone like Verner.

Yeah, the bombs flushed them out.

And Verner and the rest surrounded the ramshackle village, waiting for them to run through the smoke jabbering their idiotic mutant chatter. That's when they opened fire, aiming for the nameless figures. Sometimes, it amazed him to see how many came running.

Off to his right, he noticed one of them running away.

"Three o'clock!" Verner shouted to Tibbs.

"Fuck! Let it go!" Tibbs shouted back. If it hadn't been for the bullets in Tibbs' gun, bullets that may eventually find their way into the enemy, Verner would have killed Tibbs, simply because of the weak look in his eyes.

Verner took off toward the figure. Of all the ones he hated, he hated the ones who almost got away the most. This one was fast, running in a jagged pattern. Verner didn't fall for it. He kept straight on, waiting for the smallest mistake. He got close enough to the figure to be able to tell that it was a woman. This spurred him on even more. The figure darted off to her left, a little wider, and Verner continued straight.

After a couple of seconds, he cut quickly to his left, holding his gun diagonally across his torso, thrusting himself into a collision. She was the one who went down, of course.

Sprawled on the ground, panic danced in her eyes.

To make sure she wouldn't be going anywhere, Verner brought the butt of the gun down on her ankle. He circled her, the sound of gunshots rolling in the distance, the pealing screams of someone cracking up or melting down. He could already feel himself stiffening.

That had been only one incident. There were a number of others. He'd probably been mythologized as some kind of monster in their language. He never killed them. No, that was too easy and, in the end, did death really make much of a point or was it just something that had to happen? No, what Verner did was much worse than death—and much more memorable.

The girl in the other room moaned. Probably just cleaning out a wound, Verner thought.

After looking at the first photograph, Verner had moved back out onto the balcony. There were several more. All of them in vivid color. The dominant color was red. Verner dragged on his cigarette. What was it he felt? Pride? Maybe, a little bit. Confusion? Probably. How the hell had the pictures got there and, more importantly, who had taken them? It was a question that couldn't be answered, of course. It was like a paradox. Who takes the pictures when there's no one around? It certainly wasn't him. That would have been too messy.

But there was another feeling Verner felt. A new feeling. It was the feeling of inconsolable dread.

Verner turned and let the pictures float down over the city, vulgar confetti.

The heavy door to his bedroom creaked loud enough for Verner to hear it out on the balcony.

The figure that came out wasn't the young girl he'd taken in there just hours before. The only thing similar was the smooth skin hanging from the seeping organic shape inside. A row of faces descended down the front of its torso. All of them similar, none of them the same. All were recognizable.

"Someone had to die!" Verner barked at the monstrosity. Claws like razors came out from what Verner guessed were the hands.

They clicked against the coffee table.

It spoke in the soft voice of the girl he'd picked up that night. The one who called herself only "Li."

"Yes," it said. "Someone had to die."

Even though the hybrid was far away from Verner, everything slammed into him at once. He was helpless and he knew it. It moved toward him, standing at the balcony's threshold.

Verner thought about what he'd done to his victims. He couldn't let that happen to himself. He remembered their screams, remembered the way the skin sounded as he tore it apart, remembered the feeling of power as he stood over top of them. He remembered the look in their eyes—the complete absence of sanity. The hybrid reached out those razor fingers, grunting as Verner had when he thrust into those countless girls, all on separate occasions, all together now.

Verner lashed out at the hybrid, gouging at the eyes rapidly emerging from the filmy skin. Anger numbed him to the slashing razors. He braced himself against the railing, kicking out with his bare feet. The hybrid got hold of his feet and swung them around, sending Verner to dangle over the city, his hands clutching the top of the railing. The hybrid stood there for a moment, making sure each of its myriad eyes took in Verner's situation. Then, as slowly as it had come out to the balcony, it reached out a hand and gracefully sliced through Verner's fingers.

With a final shout, he fell away from the balcony, plummeting down into the cold bowels of the hot city.

The hybrid watched as its personal demon, *their* personal demon, bombed his way down into the darkness. Turning away from the city, the hybrid split apart, beautifying itself, becoming countless, becoming whole.

# THE FUNERALGOER

Thrip had a lot of problems.

He found it impossible to explain most of his actions.

He did not have a job. He did not have any friends. Other than obtaining the bare essentials of life—food, coffee, and cigarettes—he rarely ventured outdoors. Besides those bare essentials, a funeral was the only other thing that could draw him from his cramped, cavelike apartment. Over the past sixteen years, ever since turning sixteen, he had been to two-hundred and eighteen funerals. He had seen *Harold and Maude* and knew what he was doing was not wholly original but, like most other things, he could not explain it.

However infrequently he did so, it seemed impossible for him to leave the apartment without incident. Part of the reason for this was his appearance. He stood well over six feet tall and was rail thin. Normally, he clothed himself in layers of old clothes, allowing them to grow pungently filthy before washing them. Greasy black hair fell in a tangled mass down to his shoulders. He rarely shaved but his facial hair was thin, looking more like a layer of grit on his bone pale face. His so-brown-they-were-almost-black eyes were normally bloodshot because he did not sleep very well. His fingernails, which he rarely cut, were thick and jagged.

Thrip could not help the incidents. When he went out in public, he grew anxious. And when he grew anxious, he did things that were clearly not right.

Like this morning...

On the way to the Thornburg funeral, he had stopped at a gas station for some cigarettes. Upon leaving, he saw a small girl sitting in a car while her mother went in to pay for the gas. Thrip, noticing the girl staring at him, bounded over to the car and, pressing his face nearly to the girl's window, ran his fingernails down the glass, shooting a wild-eyed stare at the girl. She screamed, her face turning red, forcefully cradling the doll in her arms. The girl's mother had seen this and come running from the gas station, shouting at Thrip to get away. The woman waved her arms in the air and shouted, "Get away from her! Get *away* from her, you horrible man!"

Thrip bowed his head and slinked away. He knew nothing would come of the incident. He was as much a part of the town as the corner drunk or the star quarterback. There were stories about him and he knew the town would not be able to live without those stories. Not only that, he had the police in his pocket.

Whenever there was a murder in the town, of which, admittedly, there were very few, the police came to Thrip. And he, unfailingly, could give them an accurate description of the murderer. Consequently, a murder had not occurred in Olden in six years and, while it was a peaceful town, this was some kind of record. Thrip wondered if all of those cutesy housewives who vilified him knew he was the very same man who had put an end to murder in Olden.

He had an interesting knack for feeling what the dying felt, of looking through their eyes. If anyone had cared to ask, he could tell them what the old man dying from a heart attack felt too. He could tell them there was a Heaven for some, a Hell for others. He could also tell them about Purgatory and the endless Void. But no one asked about *that*. No one truly wanted to believe there could possibly be nothing at all after death.

Lately, however, the funerals had disturbed Thrip. The murders had stopped but another mystery had risen in Olden.

His suspicions had culminated at the Thornburg funeral. Actually, the thought had popped into his head when he had crossed Alma Bentley's grave. She had been buried yesterday afternoon but, now walking over the grave, Thrip had the distinct feeling it was empty. Under a cool gray sky, he stood in the back of the group gathered around the Thornburg grave but he couldn't stop thinking of the emptiness just a few yards behind him. Before the service was over he had pointed at Mrs. Bentley's grave and shouted, "That grave is empty! She isn't there! There's no one in that grave!"

The pastor looked up from his thick Bible and went back to reading from it, paying no attention to Thrip. Two large men in the Thornburg party advanced on Thrip, helping him out of the cemetery.

"Get the fuck away," one of them said. "You're ruining my dad's funeral."

"You don't understand," Thrip said, practically pleading with him. "Mrs. Bentley's grave... it's empty. You don't want that to happen to your father, do you?"

The man drew back a meaty hand and rammed it into Thrip's nose. "You're sick," he said. "You're a very sick man."

Thrip, on his knees, stayed there for a while, holding his bloodied nose and staring up at the incline of the cemetery, wondering what had just happened. Eventually, he rose, headed back to his small apartment in town.

That incident, that feeling, continued to plague him. He wondered why he went to funerals at all. They were all basically the same and he wondered why this was. Hadn't all of these people led wildly different lives, wildly *individual* lives? Why were all of their services conducted in the same manner, as though it could be anyone going into the cold earth? Had he just shouted those things to try and breathe some life into the funeral, to give the funeralgoers something memorable?

He wanted to think that. He really did. Because the alternatives seemed to be so much worse.

That night he tried to sleep, waking up to a shattering pain. Somewhere, someone had just taken a nasty and fatal fall down a flight of stairs, pushed by the blind hand of fate. Thrip was up the rest of the night, shaking, knowing there would be another funeral in a couple of days. But he didn't want to wait that long before going back to the cemetery.

Thrip slept fully clothed. He pulled himself up to the head of his small bed and waited, knees pulled into his chest, arms wrapped around knees, staring frightfully around the room until the cold gray dawn came up over the town. Still shaking, the meager light bleeding through the curtains, he left the bed and pulled on a couple more layers of shirts and a ratty black overcoat.

The morning traffic had not yet begun and he made his way to the cemetery, some unseen force hurrying his footsteps through the cool mist that monochromed everything.

Once in the cemetery, he approached Alma Bentley's grave. There was still a bit of a swell, a bit of a mound, to the freshly turned earth and the sod had not yet taken. Thrip stared at the headstone, not yet made colorful with years of lichen and mildew. He did not really want to do what he was about to do. But he did it anyway.

Knowing the force of what he was about to feel would send him reeling, he dropped to all fours and sort of *crawled* onto the grave, staring down at the grass almost as though he was able to see through it. Of course, he couldn't actually see through it. He knew that. He could only feel what was supposed to be below there. And he could only feel what was supposed to be below there if it was death. Death had a way of calling to him. Death, the cessation of all feeling, had a way of sparking *his* feelings until they came alive and sent a scary kind of electricity rushing through his veins.

Thrip felt nothing.

And that was how he knew the grave was empty.

Cautiously, unable to take his eyes from the grave, Thrip stood up, backing away from it.

Would anyone listen to him? he wondered. Would anyone pay the least bit of attention if he ran up to them and told them about how some of the graves in the cemetery were completely empty when there were supposed to be people in them?

No. He knew they wouldn't listen. And maybe he didn't want them to listen. Thrip felt something interesting pass through his brain. A flicker of a thought. A wash of excitement.

What if this was what he had been waiting for?

He had attended all of these funerals, drenching himself in death, wanting to gain some sense of finality to its mysteries, wanting to find some proof of something more than just these bland family reunions there to placate the attendees with foggy candy-coated memories.

Maybe this was that something else. Maybe there *was* something else after death. Some form of life after death. Maybe it wasn't all so final and bleak. Maybe there were other options besides Heaven and Hell and Purgatory and the Void. He straightened his clothes, planning to go over to Travis Thornburg's grave and see if he could still feel the death below or if it would just be more of the empty nothing that infested Alma Bentley's.

Movement caught Thrip's eye. He turned his head to see a small man standing at the crest of the hillside. Briefly, Thrip thought he was going to get kicked out of the cemetery again. He was well outside of visiting hours and although he wasn't doing anybody any harm, he knew the caretaker to be a restless and trigger happy hillbilly who had never really liked him from the second he had seen him.

This wasn't the caretaker.

The man raised an arm over his head and beckoned Thrip to

come over to him.

Thrip made his way over the soggy cemetery grass until he stood out of the man's reach but close enough for conversation and observation. The man was considerably shorter than Thrip. He wore a conservative gray tweed suit with an out-of-place bright pink derby on his head. He looked vaguely familiar to Thrip but he couldn't put a specific time or place to him. The man smiled jovially and raised the hat off his head.

"Ah, Mr. Thrip, just the man I wanted to see."

"You... you wanted to see me?" Thrip asked, finding this encounter odd on a number of levels.

"Oh, I most certainly did."

"Why?"

"Because, out of everyone in this town, I think you are the only one who would be interested in us."

"And who are you?"

"Yes, yes, I'm getting ahead of myself. I'm sorry." The man's small brown eyes blazed with a cross between good humor and craziness. "My name is Gregory Nascent."

The man stuck out his hand. Thrip moved closer and took the man's hand in his own. "It's very nice to meet you," Thrip said out of politeness more than any genuine affection.

"I would like to invite you to a funeral. You're always up for a good funeral, aren't you?"

"I go to every one I see listed in the paper."

The man looked down at the ground, his smile fading for just a second, before looking back up at Thrip. "I'm sorry to say this funeral will not be in the paper."

"No?"

"Most certainly not. Truthfully, I don't really suspect many would attend."

"Why not?"

"It's kind of a unique funeral. Would you like to join us?"

"Who is 'us'?"

# THE FUNERALGOER

"You'll just have to come down and see. It begins at midnight. I trust you will be there."

Nascent had turned and left before Thrip could give him an answer.

Something about the man left Thrip feeling slightly off, like the man had taken a piece of his soul. He couldn't describe it any better than that.

On the trip back home, he kept his head down, staring at the ground, having traveled this route so many times he didn't really need to look up and see where he was going. Once inside his apartment, he lay down on his bed, staring up at the water stains on the ceiling and thinking about who that strange man could have been and how he had never seen him before and why the man would have approached him this morning of all mornings. Surprisingly, he fell asleep.

The night was cool, dark and gloomy. The fog milked the sky gray. Not a single star was visible. The moonlight was murky but ample enough for Thrip to make his way to the cemetery. After bypassing the gates, a shiver wiggled its way through his body. Excitement and fear mingled within him as he climbed the gentle slope to the dark figures gathered around Mr. Thornburg's grave.

Upon spotting him, Mr. Nascent approached Thrip and held out his hand, "Ah, I'm so glad you could make it."

Thrip did not know what to say. He shook the man's cold hand. The others gathered around the grave seemed to be in high spirits as well. Looking at Thrip, they spoke excitedly, albeit in hushed whispers. There were maybe fifteen people in all. Something Nascent described to Thrip as a "pitiful showing."

"So what happens here?" Thrip asked Nascent.

"Well, that is why I invited you. So you could see for yourself."

"Very well."

"I invite you to put your hand on the grave. Tell me what is beneath it."

Thrip looked at Nascent, somewhat distrustfully, approaching the grave but not taking his eyes off the small man. He put his hand on the dew-slicked earth and said, "Death. Mr. Thornburg is in there. He's dead." Thrip took his hand away before the sensation of nausea could completely wrap him and rock him to the ground.

"So we are agreed upon that?"

"Yes. I guess." Thrip found himself more and more confused.

"Now, what you are about to see is a funeral like you've never seen before, Mr. Thrip. It is sort of a... *reverse* funeral."

"You're going to raise him from the dead?"

"That is exactly what I am going to do."

"But why?"

"Because sometimes the dead can't forget. Sometimes the pull of life is too great and they are not ready to relinquish control of that."

"But this is an abomination."

"Be careful of what you say in mixed company, Mr. Thrip. You never know who you might be insulting."

"You're dead."

"No. I *once* was dead. Now I am very much alive." Nascent grabbed Thrip's hand and placed it on his heart. Thrip felt the organ beating slowly but strongly against his palm.

"Let us begin the funeral," Mr. Nascent said.

He pulled a heavy black book from his overcoat and stood at the foot of the grave. The others at the ceremony gathered around him as he read in a language Thrip did not recognize. Not only was the language unknown to him, the intonations were strange and garbled, like nothing he had ever heard before.

Thrip watched as the ground trembled slightly, the grass and dirt being pushed away before Mr. Thornburg pulled himself up, dragging himself from the earth. The process was slow, Nascent's chanting oration hallucinatory. With Thornburg halfway out of the grave, a burly man in a tattered tuxedo who Thrip identified as Dr. Kittinger came to aid him in his further struggle. Now all the way out, Thornburg looked around at his surroundings, confusion naked in his eyes.

"It is not unlike birth," Nascent said. "But imagine being born with all of the faculties you had at your death."

Thrip turned his head away. He didn't want to make eye contact with the risen man.

"Kittinger? Could you lead him away? Let him know what is happening to him."

Kittinger led the man into the fog on the far side of the cemetery.

"I've seen enough," Thrip said. He didn't think he could bear it anymore. If there was one thing he had gained through his funeral attendance, it was an immense respect for the dead. Since he was unable to rationalize death in any other way, he could only truly see it as a final, eternal rest.

He turned to leave but Nascent grabbed his arm.

"Now, Mr. Thrip, wouldn't you like to know why we invited you here this evening? It seems we are not the only ones with abominable skills."

"I would turn it off if I could," Thrip said. "Please let go of my arm."

Nascent gripped stronger. Others from the funeral gathered around him.

"One of the interesting things about death, Mr. Thrip, is that the deceased never really remember what death feels like. We don't even remember exactly how it was that we died. Can you imagine having those gaps in your life... in your life after death?"

"I don't know what you're getting at."

"I think you do know what we're getting at. I want you to come with us. I want you to tell us the stories of our deaths."

"I can't do that."

"You don't have a choice. And... Yes. There's something else."

"Just let me leave."

"I can't let you leave. If I let you leave, then I don't get to hear the story of my death. Nor do I get to fulfill my life's work."

"What is your life's work?"

Nascent gripped Thrip's other arm, pulling him closer to his gaunt dead face.

"Look closely. Think back about six years."

Thrip studied the man's face, recognition flooding him. Thrip remembered being in the body of a twenty-year-old woman, staring at the face in front of him as the life left her. At the time, the face was a little thinner, a little hairier...

"Oh God," Thrip said.

"That's right. She was not the first. She was merely the apex. I had developed quite a taste for murder and you stopped that. Well, you stopped *me*... The taste is still very much there."

More and more of the incident flooded back to Thrip. The girl's murder had not been quick and painless. It was the most drawn out, excruciating death he had ever experienced, keeping him awake for two days while some hidden part of his psyche felt it all. The man had kept the woman blindfolded the entire time but, at the end, during the last few seconds of her life, he had removed the blindfold. Thrip felt stupid for not realizing who Mr. Nascent was from the beginning. But, aside from the surface physical differences, the context was completely different. Like seeing one of your grade school teachers in the grocery store. Besides, he had spent years trying to forget that face, trying to forget that entire episode, just like he did after every death. Most of the time, he could even manage to forget the name of the deceased. But not this time. Melinda Kendrick. The name stuck with him, always somewhere in the back of his mind.

"You're a monster," Thrip said.

"Oh, that was just the beginning."

Thrip struggled to get away but Nascent's grip proved to be almost supernaturally strong and Thrip was not exactly powerful to begin with. There were others surrounding him, grabbing him, others every bit as strong as Nascent. The more he struggled, the harder they gripped.

"The best part of this whole death business," Nascent said. "Is that, the more people we kill, the stronger we grow, the greater our numbers."

As a whole, the funeral party dragged Thrip into the woods behind the cemetery. And there, they made him repeat the stories of their deaths. Most nights, Thrip was only able to get through one story. The stories left him bereft of nearly everything except sorrow. He ritualistically collapsed onto the ground, weeping and shaking, wanting desperately to be away from these people, wanting to get beyond the cemetery gates so he could breathe a single breath of life. And each night, the strange tribe claimed another victim, bringing them from all over the country but always making sure they died within the borders of the town, within the perimeter of Thrip's knowledge. The Olden Memorial Cemetery had long since been used up. Now there were only the new arrivals and the ones they murdered themselves. Their reach was staggering.

The dead had no concern for him, using him only for the individual stories of their deaths. And the stories were always told on an individual basis, the deceased and Thrip, away from the ear shot of all the others because, in the end, death was a very personal thing. The deceased were given a gun to shoot Thrip with if he tried to get away. They were instructed not to shoot with intentions of killing.

Afterwards, the gun passed like a morbid baton, they gathered around one another, some exchanging their new found information and wondering if death would find them a second time. They speculated on how they would take the next victim, inventing new ways so the story would always be entertaining. In a way, Thrip thought, they told the stories themselves.

Soon, Thrip begged them to kill him. He refused to eat so they beat him until he did so. Nascent told him they could not let him die. Once they killed him, Nascent said, all of the stories would go with him, along with the memories of his own death.

And, of course, Thrip thought of other ways to die besides starvation. Like escaping just long enough to take his own life. Or removing his tongue and then his hands so he couldn't write the stories down. But they guarded against this. He was watched at all times. And there he stayed, in their keep, waiting for insanity or a natural death to claim him so that he could, for once, be done with death. Then he thought about what Nascent had said about all the dead retaining the faculties they had gained in life. And Thrip knew they would continue to keep him around. His "gift" would not leave him. He would have to escape.

Months later, a man named Alex Kendrick died from complications due to liver cancer. One night thereafter, the man came to Thrip to learn of his death. Thrip sat on an old tombstone by a small fire, still shivering. He was always cold these days.

Kendrick was a thin man, ravaged by his disease and, perhaps, Thrip thought, he was haunted long before that. He sat down across the fire from Thrip.

"So, I'm sure it was the cancer..." Kendrick began. "I just want to know if my wife was there. Was she holding my hand? Did she say anything?"

Surreptitiously, Thrip surveyed the surroundings. "You know," he said. "This doesn't have to be the end. This doesn't have to be your afterlife."

"What other option do I have? Lying in a hole in the ground until the worms come?"

"The afterlife is whatever you thought it would be before these... ghouls came and dug you up."

"It's too late for philosophy, I'm afraid," Kendrick said.

"Did you have a daughter named 'Melinda'?"

Kendrick's eyes grew wide.

"Yeah. How did you..."

"She was murdered, wasn't she?"

"Yeah, she most definitely was. It was a tragedy. So young. So beautiful." Thrip knew the man would have cried if the dead were capable of tears.

"I can tell you who did it."

"I already know who did it. His name was Gregory Nascent. He killed a number of people in this area and... Hey, are you the one who tipped off the cops?"

"I am," Thrip said, wishing he could feel good about it. "And I guess you haven't exchanged names with all of your... cronies, yet?"

"There seem to be an awful lot of us. Soon we'll outnumber the living."

It was true. There must have been nearly a thousand of them now. They had moved from the surface of the woods to an elaborate underground city beneath the cemetery. Odd that they would choose a place so similar to where they would still be if they had never risen.

"The man who killed your daughter is there. I'm sure you'll meet him eventually. I can describe him to you if you let me go."

"I can't let you go. They've told me what happens if I let you go."

"What? They kill you?"

"Something like that."

"But maybe that's not such a bad thing."

"I don't know. I know that now, I'm able to walk around, I'm able to experience life."

"Have they told you about the murders yet? About how they go out hunting at night? Why do you think there are so many of them? They get you hooked on this perverse life after death and they bleed everything else from you. They wouldn't let you strike out and do what you want. So kill their leader and become their new leader. Tell them what they have to do."

Kendrick looked at the ground, ran a hand across the stubble on his gray cheek.

"How many people get the chance to avenge a loved one's

murderer with no repercussions? You're beyond the law now. All you have to do is let me walk through those gates."

Kendrick took a deep breath.

"And I suppose I'll never know what happened before I died?"

"Do you really want to know? It's never as good as you want it to be."

Freedom was so close. Thrip could feel it in his cold, thin fingers.

"If I saw him, I would recognize him," Kendrick said. "And then I would take him apart. I don't really need you. If I let you go, it'll be like bringing a house of cards down on myself."

"So you really think you'll recognize him?"

"How could I forget? You know, I was there, when they put the needle into his arm. He looked happy. That face is in my brain for good. Definitely. I couldn't forget him."

"Mr. Kendrick!" a voice called out from behind Thrip.

Nascent.

"Others are waiting, good sir!" Nascent said.

"Recognize *him*?"

"Of course, that's the man who resurrected me."

By this time Nascent was standing next to Thrip.

"He's out of context. Look closely," Thrip said.

"Closely at what?" Nascent asked but, as though he knew what they had been talking about, his hand clamped around Thrip's thin arm. Thrip would have pulled away if he had the strength.

"Nothing," Kendrick said.

"One does not ask a person to look closely at nothing, Mr. Kendrick."

"You know all of the stories, don't you?" Kendrick asked. "Even the private ones?"

"Of course not."

"But you listen in. Like you were just now."

"Only because you're a special case."

"Why?"

Thrip felt like a third wheel. Kendrick hadn't believed him.

Thought for sure he would recognize his daughter's killer. He was trying to get Nascent to confess himself.

"Oh, I think you and I both know, don't we, Mr. Kendrick?"

"By the way," Kendrick said. "I don't think we've been properly introduced yet. You know my name, probably read it right off the headstone, but I didn't get yours."

"Would you like to guess?" Nascent said.

"Rumpelstiltskin?" Kendrick said. Thrip almost laughed.

"Close," Nascent said.

And the night exploded in gunfire and pain.

A bullet tore into Thrip's upper arm where Nascent had held him. But Nascent's hand had been torn to gore, along with part of Thrip's arm.

Everything in slow motion, Thrip turned to see Nascent staring at Kendrick. Nascent held the stump of his left wrist out before him. Thrip was already moving away, out of this chamber and toward the surface. He hoped no one tried stopping him. The gun fired continuously behind him.

By the time he reached the cemetery gates, Thrip felt, for the first time, what it was like to feel someone die a second time. Once safely outside the gates, he collapsed onto the ground, reeling with the vast torment of Nascent's afterlife. If the man had escaped death once, Thrip didn't see how he was going to escape it a second time. Not with his body as torn apart as his soul.

Thrip watched the dawn gray the dark purple of the sky. His first dawn in months. He picked himself up from the ground, damp with dew, and went in search of a convenient store. He desperately needed a cigarette.

# THE NIGHT THE MOON MADE A SOUND

Walt Ferryman woke up around five in the evening. There wasn't a need to put on his clothes since he'd apparently fallen asleep in them. He sat on the edge of his small single-sized bed without head or footboard, rubbed his rough hands together between his knees, and surveyed the chaos of the house in the dying sunlight. "House" really wasn't the right word for it. "Room" best described it. From where he sat on the bed, he could see the entire place, even the bathroom, its door wide open just three feet from the foot of his bed. He smiled slightly to himself, deciding the situation was too sad to warrant a chuckle. *That's right*, he remembered, *I had to go to the bathroom to puke before I went to bed.* Otherwise, he would have been too terrified to leave the door open. He knew that the squeaky things could only get through if the door was open. Even if it was just a crack. But the alcohol had taken the squeaky things to sleep with him.

Had there been blood in the puke?

You bet. He knew without looking. It was the same as his shit. The blood seemed to be coming from all of his major orifices these days.

He bent down to grab his dusty brown work boots from underneath the bed, only slightly expecting a squeaky thing to graze his fingertips. When his hand hit nothing but cobwebby air, he realized he was still wearing his boots. And, best of all, his hand came away unscathed. He stood up and arched his back, crossing the littered floor to the kitchen area at the front of the room. Grabbing a speckled glass from the sink and some milk from the refrigerator, he filled the glass half full. Then he reached under the sink for the bottle of grape Mad Dog and poured that in with the milk. He turned a burner on atop the gas range, pulled a crumpled Pall Mall from his shirt pocket, placed it between his dry lips and lowered his head to the burner, inhaling greedily like he was sucking liquid through a straw. The first smoke of the day filled his lungs and he took the glass in his hand, relishing its coolness. He leaned against the counter and looked through the partially raised and seriously askew yellowed blinds at the steaming paper mill across the street.

He had stopped noticing the stink of it a long time ago.

Now he smelled different things. Unseen things. Unseen things that smelled like meaty decay. He smelled these odors on the breath of the squeaky things, pressing down on his chest and smiling down at him while he slept, leaving before he could open his eyes.

He took another drag from his cigarette and downed the glass. He was a firm believer in the hair of the dog. If he was a believer in doctors, or if he had the money to go see one, the doctor could have told him he was rotting from the inside and nothing could put him back together again. The milk and cheap wine hit his stomach, sending up a squall of pain from his gut and a peaceful white cloud in his head. Could the doctors tell him about the squeaky things?

"Gahdamn," he mumbled, raking a large hand across the grit of dried sweat on his face. With his callused middle finger, he scraped some sleep from his eyes.

He thought about cleaning up the room and decided he'd rather take a walk in the bloody diarrhea of the sunset first. He knew he could clean the room, make it spotless, and it would be a mirror image of its current disheveled state come tomorrow. *That's the nature of life*, he thought. Every day was like being raped up the ass with a hot poker prick. Anger surged up through him, coming from some great nowhere. He turned and threw the glass toward the back of the room where it shattered, not nearly loud enough, against the wall. He would be gone by the time Ms. Davenport came over to ask him what the heck he was doing over here.

Sometimes it took this anger to get him moving. He dropped his cigarette into a coffee cup in the sink and headed out into the evening.

The coastal evening was usually, by turns, balmy or cold. Sometimes, like tonight, it was both. There was warmth in the air, a summer kind of smell pervaded by the ubiquitous odor of the sea's brine. Yet, from within that comforting balm came a stabbing wind that made Walt think of the scary isolation deep out in the ocean, miles away from safety. It was an abstract notion. He had never been out to sea. He was, in fact, terrified to step foot into the ocean. He imagined all those hard-shelled squeaky things, rolling under the unfeeling water, waiting for the meat to come. But Walt liked to go sit on the benches that sank into the sand on the beach. He liked to feel the sun at his back and wish he lived in the West, where the sun could scorch his eyes before drowning itself in the Pacific only to be resurrected as a ghostly moon. Maybe after scorching his eyes it would melt his brain. Melt it clean away until it ran out of his ears.

Walt also liked the company of Janey, who was six.

Walking down Factory Road toward the beach, past the flumpingly noisy paper mill, he wondered if the factories contained thinking men who operated unthinking machines or if the machines had turned the men into mindless drones. He thought about his callused hands and melting intestines and wondered if he still had a brain. Maybe so, he thought. But what was the use of a brain if he tried to shoot it out every night? What was the use of a brain if it couldn't tell him the squeaky things didn't exist?

He hoped Janey would be there.

It took him about twenty minutes to get down to the beach and when he did, the sun was gone. All the gold had left the beach and the ocean and everything around it was twilit and spectral. The sun had taken its heat with it and there was now only the persistent, unrelenting wind and the crash of the gray waves, each one slightly colder than the last, Walt was sure.

No Janey.

Not yet, anyway.

He sat down on a bench and lit up a cigarette. It took him a couple of tries to get it lit all the way. He finally got it by cupping his hand over the flame and hunching down until his head was nearly buried between his knees. He pulled his thin jacket around him, crossed his legs and sat back on the bench, lost in his thoughts. His thoughts mostly consisted of thinking about not thinking.

The sky darkened like beaten flesh. The ocean, darkening with the sky, went from the color of ash to the color of oil. His cigarette burnt itself out in the yellowed tips of his fingers and he didn't bother tossing it off to the side.

The sand crunched behind him and he turned to his left.

"Hi there," Janey said.

"Whoa, ya scared me." Janey wore a plastic gray and white wolf mask. "I thought it was a…"

"Wolf, huh?" Janey said before growling at him.

Besides the mask, Janey wore a blue dress and no shoes. The mask was new to Walt, but the blue dress and absence of shoes were constants.

"How ya doin?"

"Great!"

"Ain't ya cold?"

# THE NIGHT THE MOON MADE A SOUND

"Why should I be cold, Mr. Silly?"

"It's windy and… *cold.*"

"I guess I can't feel it. Feels good to me." She spread her arms out and ran in a tight circle around the sand, making a sound like she was enjoying a fine summer day.

"Hey, Mr. Silly," she said. "You know what I am?"

"A big bumblebee?"

"No, silly, a wolf." She growled again. "Know what?"

"Whut?"

"I'm six."

"*Really?*"

"Honest." She growled and moved closer to Walt. "You smell funny."

"Jeez, that ain't a nice thing to say."

"You smell like the poison."

He chuckled. "Yeah, girly, guess I prob'ly do." He reached out to pat the top of her sandy brown hair and quickly withdrew his hand.

He had touched her once before, helping her up after she had fallen down in the sand, and it had sent a wave of nausea through him with enough strength to make him run to the water's edge and vomit until it felt like the next thing to come up would be his stomach.

There had been something else, too. Something besides the nausea. There had been an image. But it was too fleeting to tell what it was.

"That's okay," she said. "My dad drank the poison sometimes too. But I don't think he drank it quite as much as you do. And I don't think it was the same kind of poison."

"He stop drinkin it?" He tried to make visual contact with the sparkling blue eyes behind the mask but she looked up at the sky.

"I dunno," she said.

"Why'nt ya know?"

"I don't see him much, anymore. Boy, the moon sure is big."

Walt looked up at the sky. "It sure is," he said. "Why'nt ya see your dad much? Don't he live with you and your mom?"

"He lives with my mom, but I think he's getting ready to move out."

"Don't you live with em? Your mom and dad?"

Janey skipped off into the darkness and then skipped back. "Sometimes, I guess."

"Whaddya mean, 'sometimes'?"

"Well, sometimes, I'm in the house. I can see Mom and Dad, but I don't think they can see me." Janey growled and raised her right hand like an injurious paw.

"Why'nt ya think they can see ya?"

"Cause, that's why I think Dad's leavin Mom. He always cries and talks about how much he misses me. I keep wantin to tell him that I'm right there. But he's a big sillyhead. He can't hear me."

Clarity wasn't something Walt really thought too much about. Most of his life had been spent trying to dull that clarity a little bit. But that night, talking to Janey, he felt completely invaded with clarity. It wasn't something he welcomed. No, it was like a knife to the back, something cold and real and very much there.

On previous visits, Walt had thought of Janey as an adventurous girl with slightly irresponsible parents. Now he saw her as something else. Like maybe there was something she was trying to tell him but couldn't because...

*Because she doesn't know what happened herself.*

Maybe there was some other way of finding out.

*The time you touched her.*

*That nauseous feeling and that other thing. Something indescribable. A vision. Was it a vision?*

*No. No. Just a flash of red. Something else. Something sickening. The squeaky things.*

That blade of clarity again, running down his back right alongside his spine. He pulled his jacket around himself and that's when he first heard the moon make a sound. Walt looked up at its unwavering, luminous placidity. There it was again. A low, slobbery sound like a dog that wants in some place and presses its muzzle to the crack in the door, slowly panting a pant infused with just enough brainless desperation for you to feel sorry for it.

"Shit," Walt thought, maybe even mumbled, and dropped a hand across his face.

He took out another cigarette and lit up. The wind had died down and it was a little easier this time.

Janey, who had been lightly skipping around the bench, trying to capture Walt's attention, stopped and tapped him on the shoulder with a small finger. Walt flinched.

"Christ, don't do that!"

"Did I scare ya?"

"No." *It's that feeling*, he thought. "Yeah, maybe a little. Old man like me. You gotta be careful. Heart could pop like a firecracker."

"Bam!" Janey shouted.

"Yeah. *Bam*'s right."

There was a trace of that feeling when Janey had tapped him on the shoulder. Of course, it was very brief contact and he felt it through two shirts and a jacket. When he had helped her up, he had pulled her up by her sweaty little hand.

"You wanna take a walk, Mr. Silly?"

"Not just yet. You let me set here for a minute or two. Finish this here smoke."

"You really shouldn't smoke. Mom says it'll give ya cancer."

"She's right, of course. I find it enjoyable. I don't really care bout cancer."

"If you get cancer, you'll die."

"Only if God wants me to. Some people live with cancer all their life. Sometimes, the cancer just up and goes someplace else."

"I don't think you got cancer yet. But I think you're sick."

"Me too, Janey. Me too. I think I'm pretty bad sick."

"I hope you don't die."

"We all die someday. Got to. It's God's will."

"Why do you think God does that?"

"Don't rightly know, I guess. Maybe he needs the comp'ny."

"May*be*," Janey laughed. "Seems kinda mean."

"Maybe. At least there ain't so many people to deal with."

"You think it's scary to be dead?"

"Don't rightly know. Guess it would be if there wun't no one there with ya. Like if ya just died and *poof*, that was it, you was all alone."

Again, the knife of clarity entered his skin, snaking in at the base of his skull.

The moon made another sound. There was no mistaking this with the sound of the ocean.

"Yeah. I get lonely sometimes," Janey said.

"Me, too."

He tossed the cigarette out toward the water and hopped up. He took off his jacket and tossed it onto the empty bench.

"You ever play Tag, Janey?"

"Of course, big silly." She reached out and smacked his forearm. "Tag! You're it!"

He winced. He felt a squeaky thing take off up his arm. He looked for it but it was gone. Janey took off running in the darkness. A vision rushed through Walt's head. He tried to retain the vision as he took off racing after Janey. It was hard to run on the sand, a task he hadn't tried since he was a kid. In his head, he saw an empty street filled with ominous black snake alleyways.

He wouldn't have reached her to tag her if she hadn't doubled back toward him, trying to jaunt past.

"Bench is base!" she called. But not before Walt could loop out one of his long arms and tap her on the forearm. The squeaky things raced up his back on dagger legs.

"Yer it," he wheezed, attempting to run off into the darkness from which Janey had come. There was another vision, this one a little longer, a little clearer. And again there was the sickening nausea, screaming through his head and guts, threatening to drop him to his knees.

# THE NIGHT THE MOON MADE A SOUND

Squeaky things. Bad visions. Nausea. Why the hell was he doing this?

In this vision, Walt saw a low black car. It was a model that he didn't recognize. The car was an older one, but maintained perfectly. *Restored,* he thought as Janey crept up behind him and smacked the back of his dangling hand, sending a horde of squeaky things shooting up his pantlegs.

"You're it!" she shouted. Then: "You shoulda touched base."

He coughed, nearly falling to his knees. The sensations were harder to deal with when they came back to back like that, almost overlapping.

Walt felt his stomach come up and managed to suppress it back down, swallowing the puke before he tasted it.

He looked up at the moon. More than whimpering, it howled softly.

The vision was this time accompanied by a marrow-scraping feeling of panic. It felt like *him* standing on that curb and watching the restored car, but he knew it was Janey. The visions were seen through Janey's eyes, or had been so far. The car door opened and a hand reached out. Walt turned to run, as Janey in the vision, as himself there on the beach.

Janey circled around him, knowing he couldn't catch her on his own. He reached out and tagged her elbow, giving it a little squeeze in the process. The feeling, the vision that accompanied it was so strong he couldn't even yell, "You're it!"

A squeaky thing, he was sure, sliced at the back of his neck.

The moon howled, a deep guttural sound blossoming into something nearly metallic.

He went down on one knee, vomiting into the sand before collapsing onto his back.

In the vision he, as Janey, turned to run from the man getting out of the car but there was another man, a thicker man, standing right behind her, waiting. Something went over her head, turning the world to black. From inside the blackness came spinning thoughts of panic and doom. There was an impact, something blunt hitting her head and Walt came out of her head. No longer Janey in the vision, he became some omniscient eye—maybe a ladybug on the ceiling of the car, maybe a bird perched on the trunk, staring intently through the tint of the windows. What he saw was shocking. It brought on another wave of nausea. He turned his head and vomited down the side of his face.

The people in the car with Janey weren't exactly human. They weren't like anything Walt had ever seen. Boil-covered skin stretched too tightly over the expansive bones of their faces. Their eyes were too clear, too liquid to really be eyes. And when they stuck their reptilian tongues out to lick their thin lips, their teeth were large and sharp and yellow. And then he saw the squeaky things. Images lent to the sounds that had infected him since childhood. Something like bloated cockroaches with legs that were too thin and antennae that were too long, fat swollen sacs sagging behind their mid-sections. They came out of the men's mouths, crawled from the cuffs of their suits, swarmed over Janey.

"Oh God," Walt whispered to himself as he heard their thirsty suckling.

He looked up at the moon. It seemed whiter now than it had earlier. He thought it seemed, somehow, angry. The sand felt like a welcomed mattress beneath him.

Janey moved closer to him, her wolf mask eclipsing the moon.

"I guess Tag's over, huh, you big sillyhead?"

"I tried, girly-girl. I tried."

"C'mon. I'll help ya up. You remember that time you helped me up?"

"Don't recall." He stuck out his hand, bracing himself.

Janey wrapped her little hand around his big hand.

The moon screamed bloody murder.

Nausea gnawed at Walt's soul but blossomed into a kind of ecstatic knowledge. He had the answer now.

He got to his feet, the latest vision burning just behind his eyes.

# THE NIGHT THE MOON MADE A SOUND

He saw Janey from above. She lay on the ground and from the impossible cant of her head and limbs, her overall *deflatedness*, he knew she was dead. And then, spilling over the vision was the blood and the squeaky things—all over Janey, all over the trees surrounding her, all over the fallen leaves on some unknown forest floor.

"That was real fun, Mr. Silly," she said. "I guess I better go now."

Walt stood silently and watched as the little girl walked toward the ocean, toward her lonely purgatory. He watched as the water crept up to her waist. He watched as she became somehow less substantial.

"Janey!" Walt called.

She stopped and turned her wolf face toward him.

"You want some comp'ny?" he shouted, already walking toward the ocean.

She stood still until he reached her. "You know where we're going?" she asked.

"Nope. I got a question for ya, though. You ever hear of the squeaky things?"

She looked at him, the moon lighting off the blue of her eyes. He saw something like a flash of recognition. Maybe it was a look of fear.

"They any squeaky things where we're goin?"

"No," Janey said, shaking her wolf mask from side to side.

"Then I'm all fer it."

"You'll be my company."

"That's right," Walt said, waiting for the ocean to rise up through his nose and suffocate the squeaky things away.

Together, they walked out into the ocean, toward a moon that had never been quieter.

# Other Grindhouse Press Titles

#006 – *A Life on Fire* by Chris Bowsman
#005 – *The Sorrow King* by Andersen Prunty
#004 – *The Brothers Crunk* by William Pauley III
#003 – *The Horribles* by Nathaniel Lambert
#002 – *Vampires in Devil Town* by Wayne Hixon
#001 – *House of Fallen Trees* by Gina Ranalli
#000 – *Morning is Dead* by Andersen Prunty

9 780984 969203